# WIND DANCER

## ADVENTURE, MYSTERY AND MAD SCIENCE

## RAVEN BOND

IMPISH PRESS

SHORELINE, WASHINGTON, USA 2015

Published by Impish Press, Shoreline Washington, USA 2015
Impish Press, PO Box 65198  Shoreline WA 98155

impishpress.com

Wind Dancer/ Raven Bond. -- 1st ed.

Mystery, Fantasy, Science Fiction, Alternate History, Steampunk / Raven Bond, Author

ISBN 978-0-692370-95-7

# CONTENTS

Chapter One ................................................................... 1

Chapter Two ................................................................ 21

Chapter Three ............................................................. 31

Chapter Four .............................................................. 41

Chapter Five................................................................ 49

Chapter Six ................................................................. 63

Chapter Seven ............................................................. 79

Chapter Eight .............................................................. 97

Chapter Nine ..............................................................141

Chapter Ten ............................................................... 145

Chapter Eleven............................................................167

Chapter Twelve ...........................................................193

Chapter Thirteen.........................................................203

Chapter Fourteen ........................................................209

Chapter Fifteen............................................................225

Chapter Sixteen ..........................................................237

*Dedicated to the amazing Seattle steampunk community*

# ACKNOWLEDGEMENTS

It has become something of a cliché to say that while writing is a solitary endeavor, publishing a book is not. Nonetheless it is true, especially of this book. Thanks to the hard work of my publishing team, it is finally done.

I would like to give a shout out to my all Beta readers, especially Joshua Books, whose unflagging enthusiasm about this project kept me going and gave me a great sounding board for the mad science. My gratitude to the wonderful Seattle Steampunk community, for inspiration and companionship, and to my editor at Impish Press, whose untiring efforts has helped turn this manuscript into something I am proud of.

I would also like to give a shout out to you the reader. If you have liked what you've read here, spread the word about it, The crew of the airship Wind Dancer shall return with more adventures soon, I promise.

Most of all I would like to thank my beautiful Ria, companion and partner-in-flight, for her love and understanding. Her belief in what I do is the wind that lifts my wings.

# Chapter One

Airship Wind Dancer, Bengal Province

Free India States 1896

Thirty years after the Great War

The airship turned gracefully through the valleys of the first mountain peaks of the Darjeeling Hills.

Her silver-gray skin seemed to absorb the sun as it slanted behind her. For all that the ship appeared huge from the ground, it was as silent as a floating feather, her blade-less impellers making a faint humming sound like many bees. Along the sides of the main cigar-shaped body a very realistic Hindu dancer was painted and beneath her form the words FAS Wind Dancer. Under the main body was a section towards the front, with windows that looked out over the ground like huge eyes.

William Hunting Owl, Captain of the Wind Dancer didn't like to be surprised, especially by people shooting at his ship. Being shot at came with the job, but still, he preferred to be the one doing the shooting. They had just begun dropping altitude to survey the wreck of their quarry, the East India Company airship Raja Goh, when the ambush came.

They had been hired to investigate the fate of the merchant ship after she had gotten off a short distress call. The big fear for the East India Company was that air raiders of some kind had moved into the northern trade route to Darjeeling. The Company had an exclusive route between Calcutta and Darjeeling in Free India that was very profitable. The thought that air raiders might finally be making it this far north had scared someone enough at the Company to pay the Wind Dancer's not inconsiderable fees just to take a look-see. Judging from the wreckage scattered about the side of the hill, Will figured that fear was right.

Will had been looking through the heavy, armored glass windows that ran deck to ceiling in a half circle around the forward part of the Dancer's bridge. The bridge was awash in the bright sunlight of a cloudless day. The lookouts did a good job of spotting, but he still liked his own eyes on things when possible. The land below was low rising scrub coming up against the mountains. He could almost feel the heat rising off the ground beneath him. In lots of ways the land reminded him of the Montana lands he had hunted in as a boy. The wreck site to starboard was as still as a lonely grave. In this harsh hill country any survivors would have made sure to stay close to the wreck, shooting flares and awaiting rescue, unless someone had already killed them all. That said raiders to Will.

He had called for action stations as soon as they'd spotted the wreck of what had to be the Raja Goh. When no attack came immediately, he'd ordered them to slow and make a landing approach on the wreck site. Although the skies looked clear of traffic, a camouflaged sky raider could strike with the man-made lightning of a coil cannon from any line of sight. Rockets really weren't a concern until close range as a coil cannon could spread its fire to intercept most projectiles in mid-flight, destroying them. Will had hoped that he could trick the raiders into revealing themselves by Wind Dancer appearing to come in fat and happy. Dancer's electronics and engines were battle- hardened better than most ships. They could take an electrical strike or two, without worry, especially with the side gun-ports sealed up as Will had ordered.

Modern airship-to-airship fighting was seen as more of a battle of endurance than a battle of maneuver; the ship that hit first and hit hardest usually won. Coil cannon made that first punch. While not as vulnerable as a grounded target would be to its massive electrical bolts, a coil cannon strike was still deadly to airships. The first coil strike would usually only cause a ship to be wreathed in a discharge like St. Elmo's fire. The bigger danger was that it would destroy the more delicate electronics and engines of a ship, leaving it to float helplessly by its air cells while an attacker closed in. Most merchants did not bother to shield their systems. Extra weight cut into profit.

If the first strike failed, repeated strikes would change a ship's hull resistance until there was either an electrical failure of the ships systems, or a burn through of the hull itself. This was where things got tricky for a raider. It often only took one burn-through to send the hellish lightings careening through a ship to destroy it, especially if the ship was using one of the cheaper lift gas mixes that were flammable. That meant no cargo and no profit. A raider captain had to be canny and have a light touch to succeed. Still, no raider would resist the opportunity to make that first strike in hopes of having an easy target.

Will had used that *conventional wisdom* to his advantage more than once. They'd made Dancer tougher than any light cruiser had a right to be. He was confident that she could take a hit from even a dreadnought and spit right back in their eye. His train of thought was cut off as he felt the vibrations of a gun firing through the deck plates. He turned to his bridge talker, Naomi, his long hair braids whirling as he whipped his head towards her. "Who's firing?" He snapped. The ship was supposed to be buttoned down, side gun ports closed so as to give a coil strike no way to spill into the ship.

"Port Hotchkiss gun number one reports rocket flare coming at six points to port. Gunner reports it appears to be telesmatic. They say it's coming from the ground, Captain!" Naomi Walters sat the interphone station which linked all the ships phones and speakers though a switchboard. Though she would never give an order of her own, it was her voice that sent crew running and guns firing, as well as relaying to the bridge reports from the different stations of the ship. She was listening to such a report even as he spoke. She looked at him as she listened, her normally calm manner vanishing.

"They are firing to intercept!"

Will cursed himself for a fool. Telesmatics were Aetherwave guided rockets, difficult to evade or shoot down. He'd been too focused on an air attack. The ship was positioned all wrong for the coil cannon to intercept a rocket attack from the ground. Come to that, he thought wildly, there shouldn't be anyone with that kind of firepower in this bleak wilderness! And whoever heard of ground raiders attacking airships anyway? All an unarmed airship needed to do was toss a few sticks of explosive out a cargo hatch at them, and to hell with the Alliance rules against bombing.

His body braced for the blow that he knew had to come, even as he tried to see where it came from. An explosion flowered mere yards off the port side, close enough that the ship rocked in its wake.

"They got it by God!" Someone on the bridge exclaimed. Will knew a moment of amazement himself that they weren't hit, shooting a 'matic rocket out of the sky like that with one projectile gun was akin to shooting a raindrop with a peashooter. The side guns were mainly useful for ship-to-ground and ship-to-ship fighting. Whoever that gunner was, they'd just earned themselves a bottle in bonus, he vowed to himself.

"Rocket flare to port!" One of the bridge lookouts shouted, "And another one!"

"All port guns fire to suppress!" Will ordered. "Drop ballast, emergency ascent!" It was doubtful that they'd get so lucky again, but that gunner had had the right idea. The only hope they had now was to rise out of the range of those rockets fast. Usually, portable rockets only had a few thousand yards before they burned out. The Dancer's gun ports snapped open and the other five Hotchkiss guns added their fire to the first, trying to throw a wall of lead between the ship and the approaching rockets. Pipes opened as the Wind Dancer's water reserves emptied, dropping an unexpected shower on the dusty ground below. Having shrugged off her weight, the Wind Dancer's nose pointed upwards as she climbed for the heavens, streaks of fired chasing her. It was now a race.

Throughout the ship, people scrambled for handholds as the deck tilted unexpectedly beneath them. Drinking cups and papers slid unto floors. Will made his way across the slanted deck to grab onto the map table. His eyes met those of his First Officer, Lawrence Rogers. Rogers was already bracing himself against the other side of the table. The older man met his gaze and simply shook his head. Rogers didn't think they were going to make it this time. Will swore softly at himself again, and grabbed the table harder, bracing himself for the impacts to come.

For what seemed like an eternity, the bridge held its breath waiting for the explosions that would tear into the hull. With merciless regularity, Sukoto Matori at the elevation station continued counting off the feet of their ascent in a monotone, her eyes never leaving her gauge. When she called two thousand feet, Will and Rogers looked at each other over the table. Slowly Will's face moved from grim to astonished. He broke out into the wide boyish grin that looked so incongruous beneath his blade of a nose, his teeth gleaming white against his mahogany skin.

"I think we beat them," he said to Rogers softly.

"Too bloody close that," Rogers agreed, expelling his own held breath. "Orders, Captain?"

"Level off, and come about. Cannon to target those launchers," Will said grimly. He'd finish what whoever-they-were had started.

Rogers began issuing the orders. Rogers still used the British Air Navy's address of 'Mr.' for both sexes, a habit that Will found amusing. He preferred to use people's first names, which was more common among the Tribes' forces, much to Rogers' private despair. Will had to admit though that Rogers complemented his own style well, with British spit 'n polish teamed up with American Tribal cunning. Together with Saira Brighton they had turned out the best private fighting ship on either side of the Pacific.

Will watched in silence as the bridge crew replied smartly to Rogers' orders, noting their responses with pride. They were a taut ship. Moments from facing being blown out of the sky, and they were still taut. Leaving Rogers to it, he crossed to the port electric lens. Dancer had three of them, and they were better than any telescope. Rather than use glass, they somehow used electricity between the two rims to magnify things. Will didn't know more than that about how they worked, nor did he care really. He knew they were damned expensive, and he was glad for the edge they provided.

Giving the rims a practiced twist, Will focused it on the distant movement on the ground. The image leaped sharp into a view of the attackers. They had pulled away camouflage to reveal a depression filled with horses, three launchers, and a supply wagon. He saw figures desperately racing to move bulky rockets from the wagon to the wheeled launchers. He looked closer.

Will didn't see any uniform on them. They looked to him to be natives who had precious little training from the way they fumbled about. They seemed to range in age from oldsters to boys barely man high, and there were enough of them that he figured he was likely looking at every male in the tribe. Will twisted the lens rims again to bring the focus tighter, and saw a figure with a beard and a long sword haranguing the others. He looked to be the local chieftain who Will guessed had probably beggared his tribe for the launchers to go air-merchant hunting. Idiot. No great loss to his people when he dies, Will thought remorselessly. Too bad the tribe was about to become much smaller due to his stupidity. He heard Naomi report that the cannon was targeting the depression holding the launchers. He nodded to himself in decision. They had tried to kill his ship, so kill them all.

"Captain to cannon," Will said, his voice betraying none of his feelings, "Fire as you bear, full charge." He paused to set his goggles over his face, then continued to watch the targets on the ground. One group had dropped a rocket and were being yelled at by a sword-wielder. He faintly heard Naomi relay his orders over her phone. The light tubes dimmed as the ships impellers stopped, the entire energy of the Tesla engines thrown into the cannon for an instant.

A bolt of man-made lightening, yards across, cracked massively from the cannon muzzle mounted at the 'nose' of the upper hull. Even with his goggles over his eyes, Will automatically closed them, turning his face away. The all too familiar smell of ozone washed over him.

The bolt struck at such speed that the tribesmen swarming over the supply wagons and the three horse-drawn launchers never even had time to feel death. Burning at three thousand degrees where it touched the earth, the bolt simply flashed them to carbon. Those remaining at the edges of the strike, deafened and blinded, were killed when the secondary explosions from the flash burned missiles rolled over them.

The bridge lookout, darkened goggles over her eyes, reported the hit. This time a raucous cheer went through the bridge, and Rogers had to call for quiet. Will smiled to himself as he looked back through the lens. The bridge reaction was understandable. Not one airship in ten could say that they'd out-fought a guided rocket ambush without a scratch. They'd be using the story to buy themselves drinks in airdevil dives for a year.

Will watched the expanding cloud on the surface. He thought he could just make out a couple of small dots riding away from the explosion, the sole survivors of their stupidity. His lips skinned back from his teeth in anger. He hoped the survivors realized what that idiot of a leader had done to them. His actions meant that the tribes' old life was over whether they wished it or no. Even if the Company didn't send punitive attacks, without enough men to continue on as they had, horse raising, raiding and such, they would now have to learn a new life. What a waste. They'd tried to attack the rich air trade of their neighbors as if it was an old caravan of camel riders. They probably thought they were brave, he thought disgustedly. He remembered his grandfather early on in the Great War against the Invaders.

Standing Bear had marveled to his young grandson Will that he had lived long enough to fight the 'metal demons' from the sky during what the white folk called the Martian War. It had been a fight to write songs of, Standing Bear had said proudly. That was just before Standing Bear had died from the horrible burns of the Invaders' heat rays. He had been one of the few to live even that long after those early battles of horses against the giant, many legged war machines from the sky.

That was before the Spirit Walker Wovoka brought the Ghost Dance to the Tribes, showing them that they must all fight together. Will's father and the rest of the First Peoples had embraced the Dance. Then they had embraced the war science offered by the White Queen of Britain to fight the invaders. The United Tribes had joined the Alliance of Nations and had fought beside the people of many countries, across many lands. The Tribes had learned the new ways of war.

On the battlefield, or in the sky, they became known by the Ghost Dance war cry, Ay Ay Yao, the call to the spirits to fight beside them. To judge by their victories, the spirits did. After the Alliance had defeated the Invaders, the Ghost Warriors turned what they had learned against the white governments of North America. In a short bloody war, they had pushed not only both American governments, the Union and the Confederacy, off their lands and all the way back to the Great River of the Mississippi in the East, but the British Empire as well, all the way to the Hudson's Bay in the North. Now, Will thought grimly, now Standing Bear's grandson, William Hunting Owl, was one of those metal demons from the sky.

Ay Ay Yao, he snarled silently at the retreating dots on the ground. You either learn or you die, he thought, but either way it will never be the same for you. The ways of your forefathers will be no more.

Schooling his face to look more pleased than he felt, he turned to face the bridge. The attackers were dead, his people were alive, and that was all that really mattered. He issued orders crisply as he walked back towards where Rogers stood.

"Come about, maintain elevation. I want to do a full circle around that wreck before we go down. If there are any more goatherds with grown up toys down there, let's smoke them out. Naomi, phone Arms-Master Brighton with my complements, and she's to form a landing party. I will be joining them." He pulled down his goggles and opened his fleece lined vest as he came to stand by his first officer.

Like most airdevils, he wore layers of mis-matched clothes that could go on and off easily. Even electric heating grates couldn't keep the temperature uniform though out a ship Wind Dancer's size as she moved from the icy heights to close to the ground. Along with the vest, Will had a personal fondness for the supple leather pants that Tribal airdevils wore tucked into their ship boots. Without the spyglass that was holstered on his belt next to his father's old fifty caliber revolver, there was nothing to mark him as Wind Dancer's captain. Everyone wore a badge in the shape of the Wind Dancer's ensign, a woman dancing in the center of a circle, done in bright brass. The only one aboard who wore anything close to a uniform was Lawrence Rogers, who somehow was always dressed in black, as if he was still in the BAN, the British Air Navy.

"That was a close one," Will said quietly to Lawrence Rogers. The former royal Navy officer nodded agreement.

"We were damned lucky," Rogers agreed in a soft voice, his pale blue eyes serious. Rogers rarely swore. "That Hotchkiss gunner likely saved the ship."

"Find out who was on that port Hotchkiss, Naomi." Will turned his head back to his talker, "Tell them they have a bonus coming." She nodded and spoke into her horn. Will turned back to his first officer. "I think that's only right don't you?" He continued softly again.

"I believe I will give them a bottle myself," Rogers nodded in agreement. "Do we know who the attackers were?"

"They looked to be local tribesmen." Will pulled absently on one of the braids he had draped over a shoulder. "If they were, you know what that could mean," he concluded grimly.

"That means that someone is likely selling modern weapons to the wild tribes up here." Rogers looked equally grim upon hearing this. "They won't like hearing that in Calcutta," he said, referring to the capitol of what was now called 'Free India'. The American tribes weren't the only ones to fight for their freedom after the war. India, once the 'Jewel of the British Empire,' was now divided in half. "Nor in Bombay for that matter," Rogers continued, referring to the capitol of British India.

"Captain," Naomi said, raised her voice, "the port gun was manned by Arms-Master Brighton. She acknowledges she is forming a landing party, and quote, 'what do you have in mind Captain?' end quote," Naomi finished blandly. Will glanced at Rogers, seeing the older man's face turn red with suppressed anger.

"Well, looks like our resident witch has pulled off another one," he whispered to Rogers smiling. Everyone on the ship knew that the flamboyant Arms-Master, Saira Brighton, and the disciplined First Officer Rogers rubbed each other the wrong way. That both held unspoken respect for the other's ability, and total loyalty to William Hunting Owl, made it a matter of amusement rather than tension for Will. Most of the time anyway, he reflected wryly.

"That undisciplined little piece of baggage!" Rogers said quietly between clenched teeth. "I don't care if she's the bloody wizard Merlin, she was off station..."

"And she saved all of us, Mr. Rogers," Will whispered back firmly cutting him off. "I think that fact closes it." Rogers brought himself up short, and then nodded silently.

"Tell her she gets two special bottles tonight," Will said to Naomi. And that I will join the landing party presently."

"Are you still thinking of going down there?" Rogers frowned. Will shrugged.

"We have to satisfy the Company bean counters the wreck is the Raja Goh if we're to get paid." He grinned at Rogers. "Besides I recall a certain First Officer who was just complaining that we needed more money for Hong Kong. The Company does pay well."

"I am not sure that I shouldn't view this new fiscal responsibility with alarm," he said dryly. He waved a hand "Never mind, you're right. I suppose that I simply dislike being the East India Company's errand boys."

"Me too," Will said seriously. "But we can wash our hands afterwards. We can't fail in Hong Kong. We're closer than ever, Lawrence. I had a Dream last night."

Rogers pursed his lips and remained silent at that, hearing the capitol 'D' in his captain's voice. He'd seen a lot since joining with William Hunting Owl that he couldn't explain. William was one of the best commanders he'd ever served with, despite his familiarity with the crew and his Tribal 'spirit ways'. Rogers didn't care what the science boffins back home said about 'magic' being real; it was still mumbo-jumbo to him. Wishful thinking most of the time that merely got you killed so far as he was concerned. Still, Will's dreams had pointed the way for them in a manner that Rogers couldn't explain. At least the Captain was discreet with it, unlike Brighton, whom Rogers found more challenging.

"Yes. Well, it would be useful if that *friend* of yours would finish the package, so that we could move on to Hong Kong soon," Rogers said to Will. "That way we could stop having to take these penny jobs just to keep up appearances." A fighting airship too long land docked for no apparent reason would draw questions that they had worked five long years to keep from being asked about their activities.

"He will Lawrence, he will," Will reassured the older man. "I believe that is the message from the dream."

Will paused in talking as Michael McGuire raised his hand silently to get his attention. Will walked over to the aether wave station. The Wave operator held out a folded piece of paper. "Wave call for you Cap'n," he said in his soft Irish brogue. "I have them on standby."

Will unfolded the paper, and looked at it. It had a single word on it, *Mouse*. Will nodded.

"Thank you Michael," he said as quietly. "Route it to my day cabin if you please."

He handed the paper off to Lawrence Rogers as he walked by. "Speak of the devil," Will breathed at Rogers in passing with a grin. The First Officer glanced down to read the note, then looked up again without comment.

"Mr. Rogers, you have the bridge," Will continued in a louder voice.

"Aye, Aye, Captain," he acknowledged formally, "I have the bridge." Rogers folded the paper into his closed fist.

"Oh, and Lawrence..." he called to his first officer, pausing at his day cabin door.

"Captain?" Rogers replied quizzically.

"You really should see about keeping the bridge tidier," Will gestured at the broken cups and strewn papers on the deck. "I am surprised by all this." This pronouncement was greeted by a few discreet chuckles.

"Aye Aye Captain," Rogers replied in his best deadpan voice, knowing what his Captain was about. "I will be sure to schedule our next near-death evasion for just before the duty cleaning."

"Good man!" Will nodded in solemn satisfaction, seeming to ignore the smothered laughter. "I have every confidence that you will. Carry on." The chuckles grew into guffaws from every corner of the bridge as their tensions released.

Will entered his day cabin with a satisfied grin. As he closed the door he heard Rogers call out gruffly, "All right you air devils, and you've had your fun now! Mr. Walters..." The answering voices came sharp and steady. Wills smile grew broader. He had remembered his father's advice that a boost to morale was more valuable than an extra Tesla engine.

Crossing to his desk, he collapsed in the chair, pulling out his pipe from a drawer. He took a moment to kindle it alight, blowing smoke towards the ceiling. He may not keep to all the ways of his forefathers, but he could offer the tobacco smoke to the Spirits in thanks for their aid today. The Wind Dancer was built in such a way that he needn't worry about a stray spark. After a moment of silent communion, he turned his attention to the call. Holding his pipe in one hand, he turned the switch that opened the repeater on his desk.

"Ready Michael," he said. There were the usual clicks and hisses as McGuire made the connections. Then a voice came from the small speaker grill on the desk, tinny but clear.

"Are you there, old friend?" The voice asked. Will still had a moments wonder at the thought of the voice of his ally coming to him live from thousands of miles away. He shook his head in bemusement. Time to stop woolgathering and pay attention. Will picked up the microphone that laid next to the speaker.

"I am, old friend." Will blew more smoke towards the ceiling as he leaned back in his chair, crossing his feet on the desk before him. He thumbed the microphone on again.

"I'm afraid that you've waved at a rather bad time though. What may I do for you?"

"Ah, I will be brief then." The voice replied. "I am afraid that the package that we were discussing as your introduction to the Chinese Spider has been stolen."

Will's feet hit the deck as he sat upright. He removed the pipe from his mouth as he leaned towards the speaker grill.

"How? When? I thought that it wouldn't even be ready until week's end."

"Just a few hours ago now," the voice said. "I would rather discuss the particulars in person. How quickly can you come to our meeting place?"

"We have to finish our current business," Will replied. He calculated quickly in his head. "I'm sorry, not sooner than fifty hours." Damn, Will thought, they should never have taken this job. On the other hand, they needed the money too much to sit in Calcutta for weeks. Besides, he reminded himself, it would have looked too suspicious to be idle for so long. Still, if they'd lost this chance to get in with the Asian underground, it would be a hard set-back.

"That is much better than I had hoped." The relief in the voice over the Aetherwave was audible. "I have begun my own inquires but I must be careful. You understand." Will nodded, and then remembered that the other couldn't see him.

"I do," he said into the mike. "Do you have any clues at all?"

"None," the voice replied unhappily. "Also, you should know that a British Scholar, Lord Hadley, has been making inquiries in Hong Kong that are coming too close to our Spider for comfort. The Spider is feeling very uneasy. I have not told his people about the theft yet."

Will cursed under his breath. That was all they needed, the Spider becoming even more leery of foreigners.

"Understood" he said unhappily. "Any other good news?"

"Well, it is not raining yet," the voice replied.

"That's good," Will smiled in spite of himself at their shared joke. "I'll see you in, oh, call it, sixty hours at the latest. Wave if you learn anything else." He paused, thinking if there was anything else he could say. Not really. At least not over an open Aetherwave connection. McGuire assured him that it would be difficult for anyone to listen in on Aetherwave calls. Will noted that the Irishman never said it was impossible.

"Owl clear," he said finally, in the traditional Aetherwave call ending.

"Mouse clear," the voice replied. There was the hiss as the connection closed.

"I'm done, Michael." Will spoke into his microphone. "Next time ask before you listen in on one of my waves."

"Uh, Aye Aye Sir," came McGuire's voice hesitantly from the speaker grille. "I must have left the switch open by mistake."

Will grinned to himself. That McGuire had been listening had been purely a guess on his part. He knew about McGuire's tapdancer past. Generally a crew member's past didn't matter, but old habits die hard.

"Understood," Hunting Owl spoke. "While you are on the line, please have Naomi inform the Arms-Master that I will be there presently. Hunting Owl clear."

"Bridge clear," came the quick response, followed by a sharp click. Will nodded to himself, satisfied. That should cure him from listening in. It wasn't that McGuire was trouble, he judged, so much as the man simply needed his knuckles rapped now and then.

Will swiveled in his chair to stare moodily out the porthole. The barren lands stared back at him. He pulled out the battered, gold pocket watch automatically from his vest, then clutched it, unopened, in his hands for a moment as the emotion washed over him.

The watch, along with his old seven-barrel revolver, were the only things Will had left of his father. He and Rogers had run out of leads to find his killers. The Mouse's idea to get them in with the Chinese Spider had looked like their best hope to discover more clues. Will drew on his pipe, remembering his dream. As he sat there, Will felt rather than heard the whisper of Owl wings over his head. The totem came when he would, but it was a clear sign to him that Owl was saying 'Hey stupid! Hunt here!'

The scheme to infiltrate the Spider's organization was still their best hope, he was sure of it. The Spider's organization smuggled things all across the Pacific Rim and farther, from the Kingdom of California to the doors of London itself. First, though, they'd have to get the package back, which wouldn't be easy. Well, he reflected, as the Old Man had always said, 'if it was easy someone else would have done it already'.

The land grew closer as he gazed out. Will had always felt at home in the sky. He took to it the way his father had to riding horses. He knew from the way she felt that the Dancer was coming down to hover over the wreck, even though he couldn't see it from this side of the ship. He stirred in the chair, pulling the pipe from his lips. Holding up the pipe to the sky, he silently thanked Owl for pointing the way. There was still a lot to do. He opened the watch one-handed, checking the time, then put it back in his pocket. Maybe, if they hurried the wreck survey, they could do turnaround before dark. He turned in the chair, placing the pipe back in its drawer, then stood up, mind still turning over what the Mouse had said in their conversation.

"Lord Hadley, huh," he said to himself out loud, hitching up his gun belt. He cursed again. Damned British aristocrats always made things worse.

# Chapter Two

Wind Dancer, Bengal, Free India

Will moved towards the main loading bay that laid mid-ships of the lower body after he had put on the prototype battle vest that the Savant he called the Mouse had given him. He was supposed to try out for a favor. If it really did work as the Mouse thought it would, then the favor would be Will's. It was supposedly made out of some kind of cloth that hardened protectively when a bullet or other projectile hit it. The vest also had many little copper disks embedded in it linked by metallic stitching. Supposedly these could dissipate the charge of an electric weapon. It was far more comfortable than the rubber armor that was commonly worn by ground troops. That armor was a defense against 'sparkies' as the hand-held versions of the electric weapons were called, though it would not stop a coil cannon.

Neither would the vest, which didn't bother Will that much. He figured that if he placed himself in front of a cannon he deserved what he got. He heard the echoes of the men and women of the landing party long before he entered the big loading bay. The sound was the good natured catcalling and shouted comments of people about to enter what they knew could be a dangerous situation. The ship herself would never land, there was no need for it. Her job would be to hover above, covering the landing party with her side guns and ready to pull them up and out if it was needed. It wasn't usual for Will to go down with the landing group, but he felt restless and in need of something to do after the ambush. He'd abruptly left Rogers in command on the bridge. He was sure he'd hear about it from the Briton officer later in private. However, as Will was fond of pointing out, they weren't in one of the spit-and-polish air navies anymore.

He entered the bay to find his Arms-Master, Saira Brighton, finishing her quiet instructions to a young man. Both of them wore the skin-tight rubber armor of a modern fighter. The daughter of a British air merchant and a queen of the Naga, the Serpent People, famed assassin-sorcerers of the Indian continent, Saira was as deadly as she was beautiful. Saira had joined soon after Will had claimed the Dancer. Together with Lawrence Rogers, the three of them had made the Wind Dancer the best mercenary airship this side of the Pacific Rim. If a captain was a fighting ship's brain, then the Arms-Master was its muscle.

Using an almost unholy combination of battle-skills and guile, Saira had earned more than merely the respect of the crew. She had earned the trust of William Hunting Owl. A man who trusted no one after the death of his father, except perhaps for a British air sailor, Lawrence Rogers. Catching Saira's eye, the dark skinned woman hurried over to Will's side. She looked him up and down.

"Think that magic vest will keep off the lightings?" Saira greeted him dryly, in a soft voice that only he could hear. Will shrugged.

"I guess that we'll find out someday." He gestured at the gathered fighters in their rubber armor. "Isn't dropping them in full kit a little much for this heat?" It was Saira's turn to shrug.

"I thought maybe that we were only going to be facing poxy air pirates when the day started," she said in her lilting voice. "But northern nomads with guided rockets? I will be prepared for any others to have sparkies as well." Electric guns were absolutely deadly to unprotected targets. Shooting a beam of invisible light that the deadly current traveled along, if you could see your enemy, they was dead, no matter where the beam touched. Will had seen to it that the Dancer had a number of the 'rifle' variety, with a longer range and longer charge than the 'pistol' type. The War had left a surplus of electric guns that had found their way into the hands of anyone who could pay. No one was fast enough to dodge a sparkie though, except perhaps Saira, Will reflected musingly. No one knew what the assassin-witch was capable of, like shooting down a 'matic missile for instance.

"By the way," Will continued in the same hushed tones, "good job with shooting down that 'matic. We would have been done had that hit us." Saira waved off his thanks.

"It was a warning from the spirits," she said easily. "I just happened to be at the gun station when I was needed." She looked out over her 'Tigers', as she called them almost fondly, "Besides," she went on as if Will hadn't spoken, "a little sweat will do them all good." She glanced up at the taller Captain. "Shall we begin?"

"Just a moment," Will produced a wide leather bracer with knobs and a disk festooning it. It was another gift from the Mouse. "I do not have a vest for you," Will said, "but I do have this. I've had Michael set it for the same code as both Dancer's and mine." He held up his left wrist to show her the contraption. Saira slung her electric rifle and reached for the bracer.

"And this will work the same as an Aetherwave set?" she said wonderingly. She strapped it to her forearm, then moved her arm experimentally up and down. "It is very light," she peered at the dials and knobs. "How does it work?"

Will reached over, turning a switch. "That means it's on now," he said. The same hand reached for a stud on his own bracer. "Michael can you hear me?" He said. The Wave operator's voice came from both disks at the same time.

"You are coming in loud and clear Cap'n," McGuire said. "Does the Arms-Master have hers on yet?" Will gestured for Saira to push the stud on hers. She did so, then spoke into the disk.

"I am wearing mine," she said. Her voice coming from Wills forearm at the same time made her eyes go wide in wonder.

"I read you five-by-five Arms-Master," McGuire responded. "Are you standing close by the Cap'n?" Saira pressed the stud again, "I am," she replied.

"That's likely why I'm getting some voice distortion then," the Wave operator said. "In the future try not to both have the send buttons depressed at the same time." Will grinned and depressed his to respond.

"Understood, Michael", he replied. "We'll talk again when we are on the ground. Owl out."

"Wind Dancer out," came the reply through both disks. Saira looked from her wrist to his. She raised an eyebrow skeptically.

"This will take some getting used to," she said. Will grinned at her wider.

"Yes it will," he said. "But think of all the uses for it in a landing. Hell, think of all the uses for it shipside!" Saira shook her head.

"I am not sure I want McGuire, or anyone else, listening in on my arm," she replied. Will shrugged at this.

"McGuire tells me that it only works if you push the button, and that the Wave will only go to either another bracer or the main *Dancer* Wave set," he said.

"Very well," she said resignedly, "I can see where it might be useful. I will wear it," She looked up at the taller Cap'n. "Are we ready then?"

Will nodded. Saira turned to the room. Suddenly her voice cut through the Tigers' conversations.

"All right you Tigers, listen up!" Her words echoed off the bulkheads even though she hadn't raised her voice. Will wished he could do that trick with his voice. Even with Saira's coaching he still hadn't gotten the knack of it. Everyone turned to look at her and Will attentively.

"The Captain here, is going down with us," she continued. "In deference to him we will be dropping to the landing area by flat rather than by stirrup and line." This pronouncement earned some soft chuckles from the listeners, while Will smiled beatifically at them. They all had seen Will's skill at sliding down from the ship during a fight. It was rumored that being a Ghost Warrior, Will had learned to 'drop' using only a rope with a stirrup with his mother's milk, which was not all that inaccurate.

"I want us all to keep to the standard formation," Saira said. "No need to go off sight-seeing. I want everyone to stay in their position." She pointed to the young man she had been talking to when Will had come in. "Ravin there will be working the picture taker. The young man in question hefted a black box about the size of his head.

"Tikku," Saira called. A rubber clad woman nodded at her name. "I want you to stick close to Ravin if we run into any trouble." Tikku smiled at the man who managed to shyly smile back. "Questions?" Saira asked. One of the Greek sailors raised a hand.

"Loot?" he asked shortly. Saira turned to Will.

"Only what you can quickly carry," he answered. "I want to investigate the crash, and get moving again. Look for the ship strong box, which the Company gets, not us." He paused. "Survivors to be taken back if we find any of course." This earned an even louder round of chuckles from the hardened landing force. They knew the odds of anyone surviving an attack such as the Wind Dancer had experienced.

"Do not take any unnecessary risks," Will continued. He raised his fist, and everyone else raised theirs in response.

"And remember, everyone returns!" The last two words were repeated solemnly by all the Tigers. It was the Wind Dancer's unofficial motto. While it might seem arcane to someone not schooled in the ways of the airdevils, it was as close as a prayer as they all came. The crew were all veterans of the air, and knew that for some ships it was a standard answer to fly off and leave them on the ground. Sometimes even dump the wounded over the side to lighten the load. Not on Wind Dancer.

"Alright," Saira ordered, gesturing to the flat hanging from a power winch over the loading hatch. "Everyone to their places, Captain and Ravin in the center." The Tigers climbed onto the lift, facing outward, leaving room for Saira, Will, and Ravin at the center of the lift. Saira signaled the Cargo Master and the lift began its descent.

The heat hit them like a hammer as they descended. By the time the lift touched down, even Will was soaked through with sweat. He hated to think what the Tigers were going through in their rubber suits. Still when the lift touched the ground they moved off it in sharp order, weapons at the ready. Two of the Tigers peeled off from the rest, scouting the area.

Will looked at the wreckage of the Raja Goh. Twisted spars curved overhead, tattered bits of the air ship's covering hung from them like burnt skin. Everywhere debris was scattered across the ground. Will pointed to a section of hull.

"Ravin," he ordered. "Catch that spot there. We want to show to the bean-counters that their ship was shot down." Ravin dutifully raised the kinescope towards where Will pointed. The picture electronically etched itself onto the thin metal spool within it. Ravin stood patiently while the scope vibrated in his hands. When it stopped, he moved the lens slightly to catch a different angle, then depressed the trigger again. He looked up at the cry of one of the scouts.

"Over here!" came the scout's voice. Saira and Will both turned to follow the voice over the slight rise of the hill the wreck had settled on. Following the rest, Ravin stopped when he saw the bodies staked out on the ground. These crew had clearly survived the ambush only to be taken by the savage tribesmen. Ravin swallowed hard, fighting his stomach at the stench.

"Get them on the reel, Ravin," Will said quietly. "The Company will want it." Saira was looking around sharply, rifle raised, as if she were hunting the perpetrators of the outrage.

As Ravin's scope recorded the scene, a single musket shot rang out across the hills. Will was flung backwards into the dirt, as the rest dived for cover. Saira stood over him and snarled wordlessly, her rifle coming up, a violet flash coming from the muzzle. Across the depression, the head of the attacker burst into flame, his rifle falling to the ground. Saira then dropped to crouch over her Captain. To her amazement, Will tried to rise to his elbows.

"What are you doing?" she exclaimed. "I thought you were dead!" Her head snapped back up, searching for more attackers. Other Tigers had run crouched over to where the ambusher laid. They straightened up signaling the all clear.

"It's not that bad, Saira," Will replied calmly, "the vest must have caught it." He held up a flattened bullet. "The damn thing has gone all stiff though and I can't get up." He held up a hand. The Arms-Master helped him up.

"Now I know that, I want one of those vests," Saira quipped. "I want to dance naked through a landing too!" Will smiled at this.

"I will see to it that you get the next one," Will promised. "Any idea who our attacker was?" Saira shrugged.

"He looked to be some cow-herder mudfoot nomad," she replied. "Most likely one of the ones who did this." She gestured towards the bodies of the tortured crew laid out on the ground. Will nodded grimly.

"Too bad," he said. "I would have liked to get one of them alive for the Company." Saira snorted, caressing her electric rifle.

"Better to simply give the mudfoot a bolt rather than make them go through all the muck of one of your so-called civilized trials. They would only hang him anyway."

"I cannot say I disagree," Will responded. "Still, it might have meant a bonus for us if we could present a live one." Saira raised her chin.

"Take anyone else alive if you can!" Saira called out. She turned back to Will with a nod.

"Should we not get you back above?" She asked. "You were shot, you understand." Will shook his head.

"Not before we see if that strongbox is in one piece," he replied laconically "You do want to get paid don't you?"

# Chapter Three

Wind Dancer, Bengal Province

Free India States

Very well," Saira Brighton, Arms-Master of Wind Dancer, pronounced, "That finishes our meeting. Good work out there everyone. I will expect you all at drill in the morning where we will work more on guard formation. You may go about your business or..." she pulled the cork from her own bottle again. "You may finish your drinks, if you haven't already." She took a healthy swig, feeling the rum burn comfortably on the way down.

With differing versions of "Aye Aye," some members of the landing party stood up to leave, while others shifted on the benches to talk to their neighbors. She watched her Tigers with satisfaction.

The landing drop had turned out to be uneventful. Save for the shooting of the Captain and finding the bodies of the Raja Goh's crew that the herders had played with, she added to herself. They had found the ship's strongbox and hauled it back to the ship without further incident. It had all been in a day's work and no one had been hurt, she thought in satisfaction. Briefly, she brushed the aura of her newest Tiger, Ravin, with her spirit senses to find him more settled than before. It was his first exposure to the evils men will do one another, and he had naturally lost his stomach over the tortured bodies. He had then straightened up and carried on, as she knew he would. He would do, she thought with approval.

"Mind if I sit for a moment?" Saira looked up at the question. She saw Michael McGuire, the ship's chief wave operator, gesturing with his mug at the empty bench space across from her. Saira thought it better to hold her after-action meetings in the mess. Everyone could relax, have a drink, eat, or smoke as they liked, to unwind. She found that the meetings went much better so, despite what Mr. Rogers pronounced.

She smiled at him, teeth gleaming in her dusky face.

"Please," she pointed with her bottle. "We were finished with the meeting. Are you not on duty though?"

McGuire nodded, sliding onto the bench.

"Cap'n is on another Aetherwave call with Calcutta. He told me to take a long break." He sipped from the mug and sighed. "Wu does make a good cup of tea once you get used to the spices and all. How went it down there?"

She drank again from the small rum bottle, and then shrugged as she lowered it. "Well enough. We had no more trouble from the locals. Blowing up their rockets seems to have sent them running. So, the Cap'n did not want you listening in, did he? Is it about our next job?"

McGuire managed to look offended, his brogue thickening.

"I am shocked lass that ye would even think such a thing. Running the aether is a sacred trust, it is."

Saira laughed. It was no secret that McGuire was, or had been, a 'wave tapdancer'. Tapdancers made their very illegal living by listening in on supposedly private transactions on the Aetherwave, then selling the information to others. Both governments and companies used them covertly, all the while casting doubts that such 'tapping' was even possible. She knew that McGuire was very intelligent; he had to be to do such things. She also knew that he had no such scruples as he protested.

"Come now, Michael," she purred, moving so that her open vest revealed more of her unbound breasts. Saira had always disliked wearing more clothes than she had too, and the ship's temperature was still tolerable for her. "Surely you can tell a shipmate?"

McGuire looked at her for a moment and swallowed. He saw a short, olive-skinned woman with an angular face and startling blue eyes crowned by close-cut ink black hair. Her body was all taut muscle and round curves. His own body stirred at her implicit invitation. Even though this was a game they had played before, he knew that she would freely share her favors with him if he ever said yes to one of her offers. He also knew she was the deadliest person he had ever shared a table with, which dampened his ardor somewhat. Then there was the whole spooky mind-reading thing, even though she vowed that she didn't actually read minds. He had grown up on tales of mortals mixing it up with the fairy folk. No good ever came to the mortals. Even though she wasn't really a fairy, the principle was the same. Besides, he thought, there was Naomi to consider. Even if Saira took such things lightly, Naomi certainly didn't. He gave a great regretful sigh and focused back on his tea.

"You can be a most vexing woman at times, you know," he said in mock exasperation.

"But it always gets your attention so nicely!" Saira laughed. "What would Naomi say?"

"That once again you've proved that I'm not dead yet, as you well know," he replied grinning back. Shifting back to a serious expression, he leaned forward, lowering his voice. "All I know is that something has gone bad, and that we're moving back to Calcutta as fast as we can. Cap'n has had Devi crank up the engines to full."

Saira frowned at that, opening her mouth to say something, when a huge hairy paw of a hand landed on her shoulder. Restraining herself from responding by immediately cutting off the offending hand, she looked up to see a swaying giant, leering at her with a mug in his other hand.

"You're the one they call Saira, the darkie sorceress aren't ya? They tell me that you like to do it as part of your spells." The giant slurred at her in accented English, while leering.

"Look here man..." McGuire began hotly. Saira held up a hand, stopping McGuire.

"That is all right Michael; our friend is clearly new here." She turned on the bench towards the drunken giant. She saw two of the rigger crew stagger drunkenly into the mess. They stopped with dismay as they saw what their new friend was doing.

"Yes, I am called Saira," she replied sweetly. "Yes I am a sorceress and yes, I 'do it,' as you say, for both the spirits and my Goddess." McGuire's face paled where he sat across from her. He knew that tone in her voice. "What is your name, tall and manly," Saira cooed.

"Olaf Anderson," the giant said with a grin, his speech slurred with drink. "I wan' you ta know that I aint afraid of no darkie spirits." He squeezed her shoulder harder. "So let's go do it then."

"Why that is a most kind offer, Olaf Anderson," she replied coolly. "I think that you should look down though."

Puzzled, the man blearily looked down to see a very large blade pointed at his crotch. He stared in astonishment, as he'd not seen her draw the knife. He froze as the blade touched his pants.

"Now listen carefully, Olaf Anderson," Saira speared his gaze with her eyes, ensnaring his soul in their entangled gazes. She carefully ignited a nameless terror deep within him that froze his muscles, while continuing to speak. "You signed Articles when you were hired on this ship. One of them stated that you not push yourself on a shipmate unwilling, remember? You may nod your head," she ordered. Olaf found that he could no longer move his lips to reply to this nightmare in front of him. In fact, he couldn't move a single muscle in his body of his own will. He silently began gibbering inside as his head moved up and down of its own accord.

"I could gut you right now, and not a soul here would stop me," she stated sweetly. "I suspect, however, that you fell in with bad company." She glanced over at the two riggers who were rooted to the spot in horror. "Is that right? You may nod your head again."

Olaf nodded again, the whites of his eyes showing. Saira nodded in mock sympathy.

"As I thought," she said calmly. "Now remember Olaf Anderson, the women of this ship, and even some of the men, are much fiercer than I, and not as understanding." She shook her head as the razor edge parted the cloth of his pants with ease. Olaf dropped his mug. "Can you remember that Olaf?" He nodded again.

"Good," Saira smiled up at him again. "Now remove your hand from my shoulder, slowly, and say you are sorry for interrupting."

His hand did so, otherwise his body would not move. Then wetting dry lips, Olaf mumbled what sounded like an apology.

"Good boy!" Saira replied with a grin. "You can go sleep it off now." She released her hold on his spirit, while moving the knife away. Olaf's eyes rolled up into his head as he collapsed on the floor with a thud. There were hoots and laughter from the other patrons in the mess as the giant fainted away.

"You two," she ordered, pointing her knife at the two riggers. "Take him back to his berth." The two came forward each taking one of the giant's arms. They hauled him up between them. "Arms-Master..." one of them began.

"Do not even try," she said coldly. Saira made a cutting motion with her forearm-long knife. "I know what has happened here. Be grateful I do not turn my eye on you. Now git," she waved the knife. 'Git' was one of Cap'n Wills' expressions which she approved of completely. Nothing in English quite said the meaning so well. The two hapless men swiftly took their burden away. Entertainment over, the watchers in the mess returned to their previous conversations. Saira made the knife disappear and picked up her bottle again.

"My fault," she said ruefully to McGuire. "I should have been here to meet the new hires in Calcutta."

"So you do not think friend Anderson will be with us long?" McGuire knew that she had been off ship for several days, but didn't ask where she had been. You didn't pry into what others did in their off-time. If she wanted to say, she would have.

"Oh, his spirit is not truly bad," she replied. "He was full of drink and stories from the riggers. We will have to see what he does with what has happened to him when he wakes."

"Well, I be afraid that you have a true challenge coming your way," Michael said looked over her shoulder, "one named 'Rogers'." He stood up, draining his mug. "I was on the bridge when he learned of your shooting feat, and he was mad as a wet chicken."

"Mr. McGuire," Rogers said crisply. coming to stand at the table. In his hands were two bottles. "I believe that your presence will be required on the bridge shortly."

"Aye Aye, Mr. Rogers, I was just on my way." McGuire gave Saira a look as if to say 'good luck' and hurried off.

"Arms-Master Brighton," he began, and then stood there awkwardly with the two bottles.

"Mr. Rogers," Saira said coolly. She raised an eyebrow at the bottles. "Two? I know it has been a difficult day but I think that you would want to make a better example to the crew. Two fisted drinking so lacks discipline."

"Damnation Mr. Brighton," he hissed between clenched teeth. "Can we at least do this with a modicum of decorum?"

"But you have assured me repeatedly that I have no decorum," she stated. "And why do you persist in this custom of calling me a 'mister'? I know that it is done in the British Air Navy, but as you can see we are not in the BAN." She gestured around the room. It was watch change and rapidly filling with a sea of profane airdevils of both sexes, all wearing a rat bag of clothes that in no way would ever be mistaken for a uniform.

"Nor," she continued, casually opening her vest wide to expose her breasts, "could anyone mistake me for a 'mister', except perhaps you."

"We have discussed this at great length," Rogers replied frostily. "If female veterans of the War can accept proper shipboard courtesy, so can you. Not that you know anything about proper discipline; if you did you would not have been off station today!"

"If I had not the discipline to listen to the spirits today, we would not be here!" She snapped back at him. "I was checking the side guns when I just knew. She shrugged, "It is hard to explain to someone like you. I ordered the port open and shot it down myself."

"Even when the ship was set to receive coil blasts!" Rogers hissed. "You know what could have happened if you were wrong!"

"I know what would have happened if I had not done so." Saira looked at him with a basilisk gaze

"That was luck, blind luck!" Rogers retorted, forgetting the surrounding mess crew. "Do not think that your hocus pocus is an excuse for not taking your duties seriously." Saira straightened in her chair, the sound a hissing snake makes exploding from between her teeth.

"I apologize for that last," Rogers said, taking a hold of himself in an attempt to keep his dignity, as he remembered where they were. "The fact remains that your shooting did save the ship today, and you do deserve the recognition you're about to receive."

"I do not want it," Saira voiced coldly. "Who would wish for fake ass-kissing?"

"You will accept it," Rogers replied equally as coldly. "First of all, because it is your duty as a ships' officer. Second, because it is the Captains' order." He continued stiffly, "I suspect that the Captain wished for me to use this as an opportunity to mend bridges between us. I believe I have failed at that. Now, may we carry out the Captains wishes with something like grace?"

Saira nodded reluctantly, unaccustomed to Rogers actually apologizing for his pig headedness.

"With the Captains compliments," Rogers placed a bottle in front of her. "He apologizes for not being able to present it in person. Ship's business." Saira noticed that the bottle was Russian vodka, one of her favorites. He placed the second bottle next to it. "Please accept this from me as well, for a job well done." He held out his hand. Saira reluctantly took it. Rogers stepped back.

"I must return to the bridge now, Arms-Master." He nodded briskly, and turned to go. Saira held up a hand.

"Wait," she said. "Will you have a drink with me?"

"Thank you, but I am still on duty," Rogers smiled his tight smile. He nodded shortly to her. "Enjoy."

It was only after he had left that Saira looked at the second bottle's label. It was a pre-war Scotch. She knew from her merchant days the bottle was worth more than her ship share for the entire mission. She shook her head in wonder. The English were all insane.

# Chapter Four

Nightwatch, Bridge, Wind Dancer

Rogers looked out into the darkness. He tended to visit the bridge in the middle of the night when sleep eluded him, which was often. The habit caused unspoken annoyance to the night watch who he knew listened on the broadwave to that awful caterwauling they called music when he wasn't present. He saw no reason to ban the activity altogether, they were mercenaries, not British Navy after all. If his nearly forty years in the BAN had taught him anything, it was never give an order you know won't be obeyed. That had given him what his mentors would have called a 'command challenge' with this crew more than once.

Like most airships at night, Wind Dancer had put on her running lights, climbing high enough to not run into anything in the dark. Rogers was pleased with the ship's progress. They had picked up a good tail wind. They were speeding along at nearly fifty miles an hour, which was very fast indeed. They might even make Calcutta within the Captain's desired time at this rate.

Staring into the darkness outside, Rogers mused that being second in command of a mercenary airship was hardly where he expected to be in his fifties. But then so much had changed since he was a young man. He had only just obtained his commission in the wet navy, as they now called it, as a very junior officer aboard HMS Reliant when the Invaders had attacked.

He doubted that anyone who had lived through those dark years would ever forget them. The incredible devastation, the hordes of refugees fleeing a living nightmare, as nothing seemed to stand in the way of the monsters slaughtering the whole human race. That is, until Tesla and the other science boffins had developed the huge city-covering Shields that were proof against the aliens' attacks. Her Majesty's Government had disseminated the knowledge of making them around the world to anyone still fighting. With that breathing room, an Alliance of the great nations had formed, building airships and weapons to take the fight to the enemy. Rogers had joined the Alliance air service on the first call for volunteers.

The following years had seen him fighting all around the world, serving with men and women from every race and nation, so desperate were the times that anyone who could fight was welcomed into the service. The higher ups had taken note of his ease with different people, so he became a liaison officer helping to integrate the airships built by other nations into the Alliance Expeditionary Force. He still had nightmares of those swarms of hastily built airships mobbing one of the great spider-like war machines, stinging it to death. Many people had died in those battles, but so had the Invaders, all of them in the end.

After the War, now Commander Lawrence Rogers left the AEF to join the newly forming British Air Navy where he received a commission of his own and an air command.

He had chosen well. As the years passed with no further invasion, the AEF had dwindled while the various nations built up their own forces, each eying the other like cats at a single mouse hole. It seemed that humanity knew no end of stupidity, he thought sourly. Rogers had never climbed higher than Captain in the BAN. He had no stomach for politics and was content commanding the deck of his own ship. He had figured to stay on until death or retirement which ever came first. Perhaps by then, he would have saved the capital needed to reclaim his family's farm in Yorkshire from the Smoke Blight. His parents would have liked that, he always thought. But it was not to be.

His last command, HMS Defender, had been patrolling the air lanes off the Siam coast. It had been the middle of the night, much as now, when he'd been called to the bridge.

A distress wave had come in from a British merchant ship. They claimed to be under attack by coil-cannon firing raiders. They pleaded for aid from any ship that could reach them. Then the connection had broken off. If they were under attack Rogers knew, a coil cannon strike had likely destroyed their electronics as well as their engines. Merchantmen tended not to shield their systems as fighting ships did. A single coil strike would not significantly damage an ungrounded airship. It would however make a melted slag out of anything electrical on board that was not shielded, not to mention the very real danger of starting fires. It was a miracle that they had gotten a wave off at all. Rogers had to act fast, if they were to save her.

They had been close to the reported position of the ship, so Captain Rogers had ordered Defender to respond with all speed. As they approached, a flash like lightening split the night ahead of them, the coil strike wreathing an unmoving merchant ship in St. Elmo's fire. Rogers cursed under his breath. Even if the ship's hull remained unbreached, the crew could soon be cooked alive from the intense energy discharges.

He tried to peer through the night, the spot lights practically useless at this distance. The raider was running in total darkness, with no lights and no reflections off the hull. It was a totally black ship. Rogers had a moment of consternation at that revelation.

How was he supposed to fight an enemy he couldn't even see? Night battles were not done for that very reason. He then realized in horror that they could see him. He'd come in with his spots and running lights blazing like a fool. He hastily gave the order to kill the lights just as the first coil strike shook the ship. Rogers looked out in despair as multiple flashes of gunpowder cannons lit the night sky directly in front of him. He'd blundered straight into their broadside, there was no time to even consider maneuver. He had one awful moment to know his ship was doomed. Then the first shell had exploded against the bridge, and he knew no more.

When he had come to, it was dawn. The Defender had floated powerless out over the ocean, a slowly sinking wreck. Of his crew of two hundred, only a dozen had survived. By sheer luck, they had found a Siamese wet ocean ship that took them aboard just before the Defender sank into the waves.

The Admiralty courts-martial had not been interested in hearing about night raiding black airships; the very assertion of it offended their sense of order. They quickly found him guilty of negligence. However in "deference to his War record," they had been merciful and merely cashiered him from the service instead of hanging him.

It had been in a hell hole in Bombay, India, where William Hunting Owl had found him, a disgraced outcaste trying to drink himself into an early grave. Will had approached Rogers with the zeal of a missionary. The Tribesman already believed in the black airships.

One had attacked the merchant airship that had been William's home since the end of the War. Hunting Owl had not been aboard, but his father had been, as both captain and owner like many a war veteran. Will's last words with his father had been over a Farley Aetherwave connection while the ship was being destroyed. His father told him about the black airship.

Will had managed to infuse Rogers with his fire for justice and revenge, and Rogers agreed to join forces with him. At the time, Rogers had known what they were attempting was impossible. 'Impossible' however, was a word not in William Hunting Owl's vocabulary. Rogers was frankly astonished at the progress they had made, however slowly, these last five years in tracking their shadowy quarry.

In the course of their early adventures, they had come into possession of the Wind Dancer. Hunting Owl had the idea that running a mercenary airship would give them not only mobility, but a plausible reason to haunt the less reputable fringes of the still growing airdevil society in their hunt. None of the crew that signed aboard knew what Will and Rogers real hunt was.

Hunting Owl was by far a better leader and fighter than Rogers would ever be. There was no shame in admitting that, the older man felt. While Rogers had decades of experience, Will had practically grown up on airships. He had also been a warrior with the fearsome Ghost Dancers who after the War had defeated both of the American governments by force of arms. It was only natural to both of them that William be Captain of the Wind Dancer. Besides, if he was honest, Rogers wasn't sure that he ever wanted a command again after that night off Siam.

The Captain was God aboard ship, Rogers reflected. He either put spine in his crew or he did not. William did. Even if the crew did not know the particulars, they could sense that William Hunting Owl had an air of noble purpose. That aura rubbed off on those around him. They held their heads up higher because of it. Hell, even Rogers had been changed by it. It didn't matter that Will was also the wiliest, most dirty fighting rogue Rogers had ever met. Far from it. The crew respected him for his cunning as much as for his sense of honor. If Will Hunting Owl gave you his word, you could be sure that he would give his life to keep it.

Will also did his best to bring his crew back alive, rich, or both if possible. Mostly he succeeded. That mattered to the misfits and broken veterans who signed to fly on a private fighting ship. They may hold their lives cheap, but Will didn't, and so they began not to as well. Rogers knew he couldn't give the crew half that much espirit.

No, Rogers thought, he was content to be God's Right Hand, as every good First Officer was. Besides, someone had to turn this lot of sorry airdevils into something resembling a fighting ship, which Rogers could do. Because what had started as a mere disguise, had become fact, they were a mercenary airship now. A damned good one to Rogers mind, but the real thing to be sure. They had a reputation as honest, if deadly fighters. Certainly they were more disciplined than most of the rabble in the air who sold their guns, which reminded him.

"Mr. Hattori," he snapped out without turning. "I believe that you should finish that log entry before the watch changes, don't you?" He asked archly. The younger man gulped and wrote more furiously, certain that the old man had eyes in the back of his head. Rogers hid a smile at using the old trick. In fact, Rogers had seen that he had left the log open when he had entered the bridge.

Perhaps someday they would catch their prey, Rogers thought, and the nightmares would stop. Perhaps then he wouldn't need rum to sleep at night. Perhaps. Until that day, God's Right Hand would keep a strong grip. He recalled the earlier debacle with Brighton. As strong as he could manage at any rate, he thought wryly.

# Chapter Five

Warehouse District, Bombay, India

Saira kept watching the dilapidated building while listening to Cap'n Will and Jarro. For days they had followed the twisted trail of a thief that had led them all the way to Bombay, capitol of British India. The next step on the trail lay in the old warehouse she now watched.

Saira hated British India, even though she was born here. For one thing, it was far too close to her mother. She had adopted a disguise of sorts, binding her breasts to change her outline, pads in her boots to shift her walk, a leather flight cap, straps dangling loose beneath her chin. She was still clearly a woman airdevil, but to a casual observer she hoped she would not appear to be Saira Brighton. Her teachers had always stressed that simple disguise was best; especially if the hunters thought they knew their quarry. She hoped they were right. She also hoped that she did not encounter any of those teachers who were still living while she was in Bombay.

If Cap'n Will had noticed the changes, he hadn't remarked on them. She had told him of her family difficulties when first she joined the ship. She thought it only fair he know that her mother was high priestess of the most feared assassins and sorcerers in India, and that mother was not pleased with her. His only comment had been that everyone had family troubles of some kind. His rule was that signing on to Dancer was a fresh start, and the past was past. If that past did come calling, he had said in his strange drawl, you won't have to face it alone. She read his heart while he spoke, she could not be lied to when she used her power, though that sort of closeness was difficult and tiring for her. She knew with certainty that he spoke truth. To her astonishment, she discovered that she had found something on Wind Dancer she did not know she was looking for. She had found a home and a family.

Jarro had been arguing with the Cap'n ever since the next informant's name had been whispered to them in a smoky den. This worried her as she had never seen the helmsman argue with anyone. Behind his fierce facial tattoos, Jarro was usually very calm and agreeable. Despite his coming from some island she had never heard of, Saira found his spirit very much like that of one of her own people, calm as a still pool, yet fierce as a tiger. If he had not been so important at the helm, she would have gladly added him to the Tiger landing crew. It had been the Captains idea that he come along today, and it had been a good one. The three of them had spent endless time talking to various disreputable sorts, and the giant's towering presence had been an unspoken persuasion that loosened tongues more quickly. Then the name 'Smeadly' had been spoken by an old one eyed woman in a hemp shop. The name clearly meant something to the two of them. She had watched Jarro's anger build, the red energy swirling tight around his aura as they crossed the city.

"This is a very bad idea, Cap'n," Jarro's face was that of a demon, the black tattoo whorls twisting as he spoke. "That man is pure deceit. Even if he does tell anything it will likely be false. Do you not remember what happened the last time we dealt with him?"

"I remember, Jarro," Will replied calmly. 'That was three years ago. You've heard what people have been saying as well as I have. If anyone knows where that package is, it'll be Smeadly. I can deal with him fine."

"At least let me kill him then," Jarro asked again for the fourth time since the name Smeadly had come up.

"No Jarro," Will replied again in that same calm voice. "If we kill him, and he does keep something back we won't then be able to ask him again. I do know how you feel, but we do this the soft way."

"So who is this Smeadly, and why do we want to kill him at all?" Saira finally entered the discussion, while keeping her eyes on the warehouse.

"Smeadly was a British gang leader being transported to Australia that we rescued from a ship wreck," Will explained. "He caused us a mite bit of trouble in Sydney Port. All this was before you joined us."

"He nearly got the Cap'n killed, and all of us branded as pirates," Jarro growled.

"That was then Jarro," Will reminded him. "Besides, I have an idea how to get his eager cooperation."

"What is that?" The Maori asked suspiciously.

"Saira," Will asked, turning to face her. "How would you like to play at being a sadistic, bloodthirsty, Naga assassin interrogator?"

"I like this plan already," Saira grinned broadly. "Can I actually hurt him?" A little bloodshed would distract her from worrying about mother so much she thought to herself.

"Well, not too much," Will grinned back at her. He pursed his lips in thought, "I will say that if he hurts a little I won't mind. Follow my lead though."

"Of course," she nodded sharply. "What if there is resistance by others?"

"We decide it as we go," Will said. "I'd prefer not to kill anyone if we can. Remember we're just after information here. Having said that, do what seems needed, but keep Smeadly alive. We all clear on that?" He looked at Jarro as he spoke. She readily agreed, and after a moment's hesitation, so did Jarro, if more reluctantly.

"Alright," Will nodded decisively. "Check your tools. We will go in the front."

They were not allowed by local law to carry guns in Bombay, but that did not mean they were unarmed. British India had outlawed guns to 'Coloreds', which description all three of them fit in the authorities' eyes. It did not matter if they were Crown subjects or visitors, the 'wog' could not be trusted with guns after the Rebellion of '85; the colonial boot heel was unyielding. Another reason Saira hated it here. She had seen too many good people bow and scrape, had seen too many injustices growing up in British India.

Edged weapons, however, were allowed to anyone. She carried her long Sheffield knives openly, as did the Captain his Bowie knife. Saira also carried an electric pistol hidden beneath her clothes.

One of the advances of New Science, Saira approved of electric weapons. An electric charge 'rode' between two focused beams of invisible light to the target. A handgun held five lethal shots or twice that many knock downs, determined by a switch under her thumb. Saira rarely used the knock-down setting, it was too unreliable to her mind.

'Sparkies', as they were also called, did have their problems. They couldn't be reloaded on the run. They had to be recharged from an electric source which meant a big generator. They could also be stymied by rubber armor, and were cranky to maintain. Given all that though, she thought they were excellent ranged weapons, as even a near hit would be fatal. The 'bolts' traveled at such speeds that if you could see the target you hit it. Standing in the shadow of the building, she checked that her charge was still up and the two guide lenses clean before returning it to the small of her back.

The Cap'n, she knew, preferred his revolving handgun. She watched as he pulled it smoothly from the holster under his jacket. He snapped open the breach, checking that all seven barrels were loaded and turning smoothly, then shut it with a snap, replacing it under his arm. The .50 Smith was not to her taste, too loud and smelly, but she had to admit he was very good with it.

Jarro mostly preferred to use his fists when he could. He was otherwise armed with a long blade mounted on a short stick slung over his back. Saira had seen him practice; the odd weapon was deceptively fast in his hands. Professionally, she approved.

"All done," Will announced with a smile. "Let's go palaver."

The three of them crossed the empty street as the sun moved towards the horizon. Will paused at a door that had a brass sign saying Piccadilly Import and Export Ltd. on it. Silently he checked one more time that Saira and Jarro were ready. At their nods, he opened the door.

Rogash looked up at the three who had entered from the front door and frowned. His boss often dealt with air scum, which these clearly were by their goggles and dress, but rarely before dark. The short woman on the right with the big knives was clearly a half-caste with her blue eyes. He didn't recognize where the giant covered in tattoos was from, but it was a large world. The tall man in the center looked like a tribesman from the Americas. He frowned to himself. He couldn't remember the boss saying anything about an Injun Tribey. Rogash pressed the button under the counter to summon the guards.

"I am afraid that we are just closing for the day, nobles," Rogash said hurriedly. "If you would return in the morning, we can better serve you," The Tribey smiled at him, walking straight up to the counter while the other ones stayed back, flanking him.

"That's alright," he said, teeth gleaming in a mahogany face. "We just want to talk to Smeadly," he hooked his thumbs in his belt and grinned disarmingly. "Only for a moment, we promise." Rogash franticly pressed the button again. No one good ever asked for the boss by name.

"I am sorry but you are mistaken," Rogash said hurriedly. "There is no one here by that name. We are closing for the day now. You must leave. Now." Rogash urged. The two bodyguards, muscled and naked to the waist, finally came from behind the curtain. They moved around the counter, stroking long clubs in their hands.

"Truly, we just want to talk to him, that's all. No trouble." The tall man said unmoving.

Rogash slowly moved his hand under the counter towards the scatter gun that was clipped there. Before he could touch the handle, he was staring at the barrels of the man's gun. Rogash blinked, the barrels looked very large, and his hand froze where it was. The short woman moved like a blur, one guard suddenly found her two blades crossed at the base of his neck, the edges not quite cutting. The guard saw Kali the Devourer reflected in her eyes. He dropped his club quickly, going very still.

The man with the fearsome tattoos growled in a terrifying grimace, causing the other guard to back away, holding his club uncertainly.

Rogash blinked again, staring at the circle of the revolver barrels before him. It had all happened so fast! Paan and Josh, the two guards, were useless he thought in growing despair. He'd always known they were, for all their big talk and muscles. He felt himself sweating. Whoever these people were, they were not the boss's usual kind of trouble. He knew that they were going to kill him. In his panic, he almost missed the Tribey speaking to him again.

"If you very slowly move your hand away from that gun, I think that you and your friends here can go home. We truly are here just to talk, but it's your choice." Rogash focused on the words. They could leave? Slowly he moved his hands up in the air.

"Good man!" The Tribey grinned at him, gun steady on his face. "Now," he said to Rogash, "still going nice and slow, walk to the door and git. I doubt that Smeadly will be too happy with you all, so if you ever come back is up to you. But do not return tonight or we will not be so nice! Understand?"

Rogash nodded. He didn't know what 'git' meant, but the meaning was clear. And the man was right. The boss did not forgive. Perhaps leaving Bombay would be wise.

As the last man fled out the door, Will looked at his companions, his smile going wry. "Well, that was easy enough. Now comes the hard part. Smeadly will have some sort of bolt hole for sure. Watch for more people, and traps." He moved quickly around the counter and through the curtain, only to be met by a heavy door with a steel lock.

In the Aetherwave serials, the brave hero shoots out the lock, which Will knew was a good way to get hit by your own bullet. Instead he aimed above the lock and fired. He quickly did the same below it, then kicked out hard. The splintered wood around the lock gave way when the door crashed open. He went in fast, Saira, electronic pistol now in hand, followed to his right, Jarro to his left.

Will's eyes swept the room, gun first. The room was done up in what he thought of as cheap flash. The walls were lavender and green striped metallic foil. In one corner, sat an over sized Aetherwave set next to a bright blue divan. A large desk sat more or less in the middle of the room. The air reeked of cheap hemp and cigars.

A short thin man with ginger hair was struggling with what looked to be a hidden door behind a bookcase. Smeadly, Will thought in satisfaction. He fired high, the round raining flakes of wallpaper and plaster down on Smeadly's head. The man flinched and then froze, slowly raising his hands.

"Turn around real slowly Smeadly. I will shoot you otherwise." Will watched carefully as the other man turned. Smeadly may be coward and a con man, but Will knew the ganger was serious deadly when cornered.

Smeadly smiled, showing empty hands and a row of sharpened metal teeth, the badge of the London street gangs. He was better dressed than when Will had last seen him. The quality of the bright orange tartan pants, and emerald green coat over a gold vest spoke of money. Will noted that Smeadly didn't seem surprised to see him.

"Well now, this is a pleasant surprise!" Smeadly said heartily, "Captain William Hunting Owl! I'd heard that you were mucking about in these parts, but I've been far too busy to pay my respects." He cocked his head to one side, "Did you kill my men?"

"No, but they have left for the day," Will replied, keeping the gun on him. "All I want is a few moments of your time, Smeadly, just a little talk."

"Right then," Smeadly lowered his arms, and shot his cuffs. "Love to catch up, but I've an appointment you see. I'm a man of means now Willy, important people to see and all that." The little ganger flashed his sharp steel teeth in a short grin. "Mayhap we can talk another time. I'll send you a Farley crystal. Don't worry about the door." He slowly walked towards the broken door, ignoring the pointed guns.

"You can stop right there, Smeadly," Will called out. "I've no mind for your games. Keep your hands were I can see them." Smeadly stopped again with a huge sigh, moving his arms out from his body. "Jarro," Will ordered, "the chair."

Jarro pulled the chair out from behind the desk, pushing it towards the middle of the floor. Will noticed that it was one of the new kind that rolled on wheels.

"Smeadly, sit," Will ordered. Smeadly sidled over to the chair still keeping his hands away from his sides.

"Now, Willy," Smeadly said in aggrieved tones, "You're not still having hard feelings over that Sydney business are you? It was a misunderstanding is all. Why I'd never hurt you, we're practically brothers we is, sharing the same Christian name and all. That's it, brothers! Besides it all came out on the up and up in the end right?" Jarro growled deep in his throat.

"Oh, hullo Jarro," Smeadly said to him as he sat down. "Still with him eh? You know you actually look uglier than I remembered. Life must be good to you." Jarro growled again.

"Jarro," Will said quietly, "go watch the front."

"Do not trust him, Cap'n!" Jarro said glancing at Will. He turned to face Smeadly, "If you play us false again," Jarro rumbled darkly, "I will hunt you down and kill you, I swear it." He pulled his blade from over his shoulder with a meaningful look.

"Good to see you too, Jarro," Smeadly said pleasantly.

"Jarro," Will ordered again, "now." He kept his own gun still aimed at Smeadly's head. As Jarro left, Saira moved to cover more of the room.

"Well, hallo there pretty," the smuggler leered. "Wot's your name then? Willy, you've definitely improved in your taste in companions, I must say."

"We'll get to her, Smeadly," Will said agreeably. He crouched down at eye level with the smuggler, while staying out of his reach. "To be very clear, this is not about Sydney. Word says that you're now the man who knows everything about how certain commodities move around and out of this city."

Smeadly shrugged, and puffed up his chest.

"Told you I'm a man of means these days, Willy. I knows people it's true." He stared hard at Will, all warmth gone from his voice, "a thing you should keep in mind." He flashed his steel teeth again.

"Good," Will replied heartily. "Then this should be easy for an important man like you. A very expensive piece of gadgetry was stolen from Shavian Laboratories in Calcutta about two weeks ago. Who did it, where is it now?" Will watched Smeadly's' face, and knew he'd struck gold. "Give me that and we're out of your life, easy as pie." The silence stretched out, as the two men eyed each other. Finally, Smeadly spoke.

"I'm afraid I don't have an answer for you on that subject, Willy. Some questions you shouldn't be asking, if you follow me. And please," he said, voice harsh with contempt,

"Don't be trying any stupid threats. We both know you don't 'ave the stones to force me. Kill me yeah, but I'm like as dead anyway if I give that up to you." He bared his teeth again.

"Well, I'm right sorry to hear that, Smeadly." Will said in a sorrowful tone. "Right sorry," he nodded at Saira. Saira gave the smuggler a very evil grin. She holstered her gun and pulled one of her knives. "You asked about my friend here," he continued, "you see, she's a Naga. You have heard of them haven't you?"

Smeadly looked at Saira as if for the first time. Everyone in India had heard whispers about the Naga, the sorcerous Serpent People who killed in the dark. It was rumored that even the Thuggee of Kali gave the Naga a respectful distance. Smeadly smirked at her.

"This little flower a fearsome Naga?" he asked derisively. "You must be slipping Willy to think you could pull that one. He laughed and then the laugh died as Saira caught Smeadly's gaze. Will saw the man's Adams apple work. He could tell Saira was working her magic on him. He sat back on his haunches to watch silently.

Saira sauntered towards Smeadly, running a thumb lasciviously along the edge of her knife. Smeadly's eyes grew rounder the closer she came. Will was reminded of seeing a snake catch a rodent, the rat frozen in place as the serpent came closer.

Saira straddled Smeadly's legs pinning him in the chair. She carefully ran the knife down his cheek, a thin trickle of blood following where it passed.

"I wonder if those teeth come out easily," she breathed at him.

"Oh God, Willy, I can't tell you, man! I can't," Smeadly erupted in terror, his eyes never leaving Saira's gaze. "Can you not understand that it would be the death of us all, you stupid Indian?" Saira stopped his shouting by placing her blade against his lips.

"First, you should know that the Cap'n is a tribesman from the Americas, an honorable warrior," she breathed. "I am Indian, as I am from India. You," she moved the knife towards his eye, "are a piece of offal whose soul I will shrive with the rites of pain, and off up to the Dark Ones in apology for your stain on the soil of my land."

Will thought she might be overdoing it; he doubted Smeadly had a soul, let alone thought much of it. But Smeadly screamed like the damned, never taking his eyes off hers. "No Willy, please! Don't let her do it!" The little ganger started crying. "Don't let her do it!" He broke down sobbing.

Will hated seeing anyone so undone, even a weasel like Smeadly. It left him feeling unclean somehow. Still, Saira's hexing seemed to be working. He didn't know what Saira was doing to him, but it was best to continue the playing.

"Huntress," Will said in low reverent tones to Saira, "I know your offense at his life is great, but I ask you to spare him if he tells us what we want to know."

"But the shriving is such beautiful thing," she crooned softly in Smeadly's face. "There is a moment when the pain is so transforming, he will gain this radiant glow, and that is hours before death lifts him away." With a great sigh, Saira stopped the blade moving. "You may speak," she ordered him.

"I can't tell you much." Smeadly began hurriedly. "I do know that powerful people are running this Willy, powerful ruthless people. The thief was the Cat, you see, as canny as they come. He says as how it was the big pay off, and would I move it to Hong Kong for him for a nice piece? They found him yesterday morning in pieces almost too small to recognize." Smeadly paused wetting his lips. "He was canny Willy, the best I's ever seen. Now he's mince, and the peelers aren't even making a row of it."

"Then that same morning an English toff with dead eyes comes to me, asking if I could still move the Cat's swag, only for him now instead. Bugger wasn't any local bloke I knows that. I swear Willy, I looked at those dead eyes, and it was like something pissing on me grave. I said no, on my soul Willy, I said no. I sent him to someone else."

"Who Smeadly?" Will asked quietly.

"A Chin smuggler name of Hu Fan, runs a sea junk called the Destiny." Smeadly said. Both Will and Saira hissed between their teeth. Smeadly barked out a mad laugh.

"I see you knows the blighter, alright!" Smeadly said. "Figured no loss to me, old Hu runs afoul."

"Tell us everything Smeadly," Will said coldly, as he squatted closer. "We're listening."

# Chapter Six

## Wind Dancer, the Indian Ocean

Will returned to the bridge with his coffee mug in hand and looked out at the sun on the water. Given their 'talk' with Smeadly, they'd rushed back to Dancer. After a profanity and bribery-laced scramble, they had grabbed sky that same twilight, mostly re-provisioned. They'd started from the point the little rat had given them, then begun a search that took them in an ever expanding zigzag. It should have been nearly impossible to find a ship in the dark that didn't want to be found. Only a full moon and clear skies plus their electric lenses gave them any hope of success. Still it was a big ocean, and night had turned into day, with no joy.

Will had taken a moment in the late morning to go to the mess, where he'd been cornered by Devi Neelam, his Chief Engineer, while he ate. Devi had been with the ship longer than anyone except Lawrence and himself. Devi looked, and talked, for all the world like an aristocratic Brahman who should be in silks and jewels, rather than the stained rubber apron and boots she typically wore. She was damned good at her job though, and had kept the Dancer flying, some-times with little more than twine and hot air.

Will wondered, not for the first time, what had led her to the airdevil life. Not that it mattered. She was good, and fiercely loyal. He listened to her for a moment, then cut to the chase, as she did tend to go on about 'her engines'.

"So how serious is it?" he asked around the last of his porridge. With the familiar pained expression she always got when he asked that question, she sighed.

"This is what I am trying to tell you Captain," she said spreading her hands at him, "I do not know this time. The number three Tesla is flexing again. It is not enough spike that we cannot compensate." she held up her hand to emphasis her point, "For now. But I cannot swear that it will not spike enough to totally burn out, fusing the conduit array with it." Will knew that would leave them floating in the sky with no power at all.

"Everything I know says that we should take it off line completely," She finished, raising her tea mug to her lips for emphasis.

"I thought you said the number three was good for another six months," Will said half crossly. Now would not be the time for a serious maintenance issue, not he reflected, that it wouldn't be the first time.

"Yes, Captain," she sighed, putting the mug down. "I was wrong."

"Look Devi," Will said seriously. "We may be about to go into battle. Can the ship fight?"

"We will make her fight, if it needs to be. But I cannot give you both cannon and full speed if we take the number three off line," She shrugged helplessly. Will thought furiously for a moment.

"Then don't." He raised his own hand to forestall her protest. "I know what the dangers are here. We have to do this one, Devi."

"Is it true that we are going after Hu Fan?" She looked at him soberly. Will studied her. It wasn't like Devi to ask after mission details that didn't affect the ship. What was she about?

"Yes," he said shortly.

"Do you promise me that you will kill him this time?" She looked at him with an intensity that was out of character for her. Will chewed slowly, and then answered.

"I don't make those kinds of promises Devi," he said gently. "If I have to kill him, I will. But the ship and the mission come first, you know that. Why are you asking this?"

"Because he is an animal on two legs, Captain, as are all of his kind," she said fiercely. "A rabid animal should always be put down!" She looked at him directly. "I ask this because I can smell that this 'mission' has something to do with your secret purpose, and I am afraid." She held up her hand as he started to speak. "Please, spare me your jolly evasions. I know that you and Rogers have some purpose other than money." She sniffed. "You may fool the others, but not I."

"No, captain," Devi continued, "I ask this, because it is possible for one to lose one's way when you are fixed on a goal too much. I fear this for you. If you make any deal with Hu Fan that allows him to keep his life, than I fear that you are indeed lost." She paused, "I will not be lost with you." Will looked at her soberly.

"Devi." he began, and was saved by the ship's chime. "Captain to the Bridge, Captain to the Bridge." He stood up, grabbing his tea mug. Looking down at her, he spoke, "You're the best Devi. Perhaps I needed to hear that, I don't know, I can't say. Keep her in the sky for me."

"Do not get us lost," She returned bleakly. He nodded, a quick jerk of his head.

Will walked briskly to the bridge, thinking on what Devi had said. It was true that while he would like nothing better than to kill Hu Fan himself, he had been thinking of ways to get the thingamabob back without a fight. He'd been telling himself that he owed it to his crew to avoid a fight when he could, which was true enough. But if he was honest, he really didn't want any chance that he would lose a chance to get his father's killers. After all, it wasn't his job to police the world, was it? He crossed over to Lawrence Rogers at the map table.

"What have we got?" He asked looking down at the map. Rogers pointed to it.

"Crow's nest just spotted a Chinese junk on the horizon, here," the First Officer reported.

"Huh," Will studied the map, sipping his tea. "We couldn't really have gotten that lucky could we?"

"We're too far away to make a definite identification." Rogers said. "Still think that Hu Fan is running that bright red hull?" Will snorted, and took another sip of tea.

"Of course he is," he said certainly. "Hu is one of the old style scum. He still thinks that proclaiming his joss is stronger than anyone else's makes him unbeatable. Let's close on her." Will snorted, and took another sip. Rogers gave the orders and then pulled Will off to one side of the bridge.

"He did get away from us at Japan." Rogers said in a low voice, reminding Will of their last encounter.

"True words," Will said. He sat his cup down and leaned on the map table, looking out at the sea. "This time though, he doesn't have a bunch of innocents for pawns."

"That we know of," Rogers insisted. "He may though, that is his business."

"Aiya, maybe." Will looked out silently for a moment. Maybe Devi was right, Will thought. After all the shady deals, the compromises, maybe it was time to actually do it right, just this once.

"Lawrence," he said in decision, "this time Hu Fan doesn't get away. If the crow comes to the corn, burn him to the water." Rogers looked at his Captain carefully,

"I thought that our mission was recovering the packet," he reminded Will. Will nodded agreement.

"And so it is. But Hu Fan isn't going to go free without a by your leave, hear me?" Hunting Owl fixed his gaze on his First Officer.

"Will," Rogers said softly, "you can't kill all the villains in the world." Will grinned his boyish grin at him, reaching for his tea mug.

"Wait and see," he vowed cockily. Will breathed easier. This decision felt right to him. If a deal could be struck, he'd honor it, however much he'd hate it, but it felt better to know that.

"And if he has hostages again?" Rogers continued remorselessly. Will's jaw hardened. At that moment, Naomi Walters spoke from across the bridge.

"Crow's nest reports water ship has red hull," she reported. Ship is underway with both sail and prop." Will looked at Rogers, and grinned again.

"That's him," Will asserted. "Let's dance then." He pushed off from the map table tugging absently at one of his braids.

"Mister Walters," Rogers called out, "Sound action stations." The chime followed by her voice rang through the ship.

"Michael," Will said, bracing his legs and staring out at the ocean waves. "See if you can make a connection. It's a long shot I know. Use our identity, and ask for Hu Fan himself. Hiki," he called to the bridge look out on his left. "Same message on the heliograph. Let's see if they'll talk."

"Aye Aye, Cap'n" McGuire acknowledged. His set the Aetherwave to the standard maritime addresses and began calling though them. The lookout clacked away on the heliograph as well, sending flashes of coded light towards the junk. Not every ship had a wave, so other methods such as signal lights and flags where still used as well.

"Lawrence," Will asked, "How long to close?" Rogers looked at the compass while measuring with a pair of calipers on the map. He straightened up, looking at Will's back.

"Unless he has more power than he should, we'll be in boarding range in about thirty minutes," he reported.

"So we will be boarding then?" Saira asked, entering the bridge Saira looked out towards the ship on the water. Will nodded a greeting at her as she came to stand beside him.

"Most likely we will," Will answered. "I doubt that he'll actually want to turn over what we're after. He'll make us come get it." He said grimly.

"And what is your station's status, Arms-Master?" Rogers asked archly.

"Oh, all the secondary guns are manned and ready, coil cannon is on stand-by, and the Tigers can muster in ten minutes," she replied without turning around.

"I thought that we would be boarding, and so came up here to see the target, naturally," she finished innocently.

"Naturally," Rogers replied in the same tone.

"Enough, you two," Will ordered them. He turned to Saira quizzically, "I still can't believe you said to Smeadly that you would 'shrive his soul' and it worked."

"Smeadly is a very religious man in his way," she replied solemnly. Rogers snorted at this.

"William Smeadly?" Rogers said incredulously. "I'll believe that when I see it."

"No answer on any connection, Cap'n," McGuire reported. "No joy on the heliograph either."

Will nodded, "Keep trying both. Let me know if you get any answer at all." He paced towards the electric lens mounted at the front of the bridge, Saira and Rogers following behind him. They took turns at the lens examining the ship which sported a wake that indicated they had an engine running as well as their sails.

"It's Hu Fan alright," Will stated, recognizing the ship. "He can't imagine he can out run us," he said musingly. He turned to his officers, "Thoughts?"

"He's hoping to keep us from closing," Rogers announced. "It's what they did in Japan."

"Agreed," Saira said. "Only this time he has believes that he has nothing to bargain with, else he would answer our hails. That means no hostages. We shall take him yes?" She asked eagerly, hand grasping the hilt of one of her knives.

"Yes, we will." Will replied decisively. "Here's my idea," he outlined the plan in a few sentences. Saira was grinning in feral agreement when he finished. "Any other ideas or objections?" he asked finally. Rogers frowned.

"If I am to direct the attack from the ship," he glanced pointedly at Saira, "which I believe we should discuss in more detail, where will you be?" He asked.

"On the drop with the boarding party," Will replied. He answered their surprised looks, "You'll still be leading it Saira. I have every faith in you. I'm going along for Hu Fan." His face brooked no argument.

"Pity," Saira remarked, hands still on her knife hilts. "I had hoped for him myself. Still it will be as you say, Cap'n. I shall go muster for the drop."

"Do so, I'll be along." Will ordered. He watched her leave the bridge then turned towards Rogers. The First Officer leaned closer to him, so that no one else could overhear,

"Captain," Lawrence began earnestly, "I strongly suggest that I not be given combat command. You should have it, or you should give it to someone else. If I were to freeze again as on Defender..." His voice trailed off as Hunting Owl fore-stalled him with a hand to Rogers' shoulder.

"It's time you did this, Lawrence," the younger man said gently. "I've watched you; I know you can do this. As my father used to say, you have to get back up on the horse sometime." He went on, giving the Englishman no time to respond. "Besides, I can't let Saira have all the fun now can I? Now I'm going to suit up. You have the bridge," he fin-ished formally. Rogers straightened.

"Aye, aye, Captain," Rogers replied stoutly. "I have the bridge."

~~~

Lower Corridors, Wind Dancer

China Sea

We're suiting up as well." Saira said to Ravin as they strode quickly down the corridor. She had met him up with him while heading to the armory. "Most surely yon Chinaman has some sparkies, though hopefully not many." She was pleased with how Ravin had settled down after his first drop.

"Joy," Ravin said shortly at the prospect. The hot rubber suits were not comfortable to put it mildly.

Saira privately agreed with him, but had been glad that Cap'n Will had agreed to the expense of the suits. Electric small arms were becoming common, and the rubber suits gave the best protection possible against their 'bullets'. The suits were not perfect protection. If not properly sealed, or if they got torn, the current could still kill the wearer, but to face sparkies unarmored was tantamount to suicide.

"Be of good cheer," she said to Ravin with a smile. "We go from freezing up here to sweltering down there. It is very good for the blood. Besides," she continued seriously, "you truly do want the rubber if you get zapped, trust me. So keep it sealed up."

They entered the armory, a room with benches for changing down the middle, weapons racked along the walls, interspersed with suit lockers. Others were already changing, or checking weapons. The room echoed to the usual banter and catcalls of the Tigers.

Saira began peeling off layers as she went, grabbing the suit that had her name above it. No one bothered about skin lasted long on an airship, there simply wasn't room. She put it beside her on the bench, and sat to pull off her boots.

"Oy, Saira!" Tikku called from down the room in a lilting voice. "When do I get to suckle those big bubbies of yours?" Tikku had started the joke upon her first boarding action. Saira, far from finding it annoying, thought it endearing in a way. Saira stood, pulling on the rubber leggings up her limbs. Feeling impish, she cooed back to the woman without missing a beat.

"Why tonight, Tikku, my light of love," Saira gushed breathlessly. For a moment, all other chatter died in the room.

The only things more guaranteed to get her Tigers attention than a boarding action were sex, pay, and grog, although not always in that order. It was common knowledge that the islander Tikku really only fancied the males. That sort of knowledge traveled quickly onboard ship.

Tikku's running joke though, gave voice to what half of them thought upon seeing Saira's ample endowments, the Arms-Master knew. Her usual answer to Tikku was a good natured 'get stuffed' in increasingly inventive language that had grown into part of the Tigers boarding ritual. It also reminded anyone what they'd get if Saira wasn't interested at the same time. This was a new turn though, and the others stopped to see how it would play out.

"Really?" Tikku had frozen in surprise, a boot in one hand. Her voice now held a slight quiver to it, and her eyes were wide as a startled deer's.

"Aiya, tonight," Saira replied sweetly. She stood slowly with a sultry smile, pulling on the rubber tunic. Saira left the frogs open until she had to close them. Most did. The rubber didn't breathe at all, and there was no point in sweating more than you had to. After fastening her knife belt in place, she stood facing Tikku with her hands on her hips, thrusting her exposed chest out. "In your dreams, that is," she finished in the same breathless voice.

The whole room, including Tikku, howled with laughter, and went back to their preparations. Saira crossed to the other wall and unplugged her personal pistol, checking that the small needle showed full charge. She placed it in the holster at the small of her back. She then chose an electric rifle from the rack, checked it as well, and then pulled the strap over her head.

Ravin, standing next to her, pulled another bandoleer of shotgun shells over his shoulder. He also had two revolving pistols at his belt.

"Arms-Master," he said to her, "I still do not see why you like the sparkies so much. Once you have fired your shots, it is just a big club. It is not as if you can carry a Tesla engine around with you to reload it."

Saira hefted the rifle, caressing it before placing it on a sling over her shoulders.

"I prefer how precise these are in the killing." She gestured at his shotgun, "Yon gunpowder cannons are loud, smelly, and kick like a mule. Besides, with a sparkie, if I can see them then they are already dead. When the sparkies are empty, why then I have these," She patted the hilts of her Sheffield blades. The forearm length custom knives had been her uncle's parting gift when she left his merchant ship to go out on her own. Between her training in Naga Darkways, and her uncle's rough-house methods, she knew that there were few who could stand against her in close quarters. Ravin shook his head.

"I would rather continue to keep them at a distance," he said patting the automatic shotgun. "I am not good with the blades like you are."

Saira gave him a smile, "True, although you are not that bad. We will see to it that you get better," she promised. "I, on the other hand," her smile grew even bigger and somewhat evil, "am very good. And not bad with the blades either." Ravin started shaking his head at this not sure if she was teasing him or not.

"With respect Arms-Master," he said diffidently, bobbing his head. "I cannot always tell when you are serious and when you are not."

"That is what my mother always says," Saira patted him on the cheek. His face actually turned darker beneath his skin as blood suffused it. How charming, she thought in amusement, he was actually blushing. Her eye turned towards the movement at the door, seeing Cap'n Will enter.

He was dressed for boarding in a black rubber suit with the battle vest over it, the gun belt at his hips holding his repeater pistol on one side, balanced by an equally long Bowie knife, on the other. Saira patted Ravin on the shoulder, and walked over to stand by the Captain.

"Listen up all," she said. Everyone quieted looking at her expectantly. "Gather 'round. The Cap'n is going down with us, and he will be explaining the drop." Everyone gathered quietly around Will who laid out a rough sketch of target ship on the bench.

"Here's the plan. We're closing on Hu Far's junk. There's a single breech loader on the fore deck, what looks to be two light Gatling's on the aft deck. No other heavy guns that we can see. Reckon the crew's about a hundred or so all up." He pointed while he talked. "We're going to steam bath the fore deck, and drop down on her there. Dancer will be angled to give us suppression fire over the aft deck with the

Hotchkiss Guns." He handed the briefing off to Saira with a wave.

"Georgios, Abdul, you will spike the breech loader," Saira picked up the briefing without a pause. The two strong men nodded solemnly. Saira continued, "Miriam, you will stand with them to cover a retreat if we need one." The ginger-braided woman patted her long rifle cockily, "You got it boss," she said. Saira nodded at her.

"I will lead one group down the port side," Saira reminded them, "the Captain will lead the other down the starboard side." Will nodded in agreement at her. She looked around at them. "You all know the way of it, we have trained for this. There is plenty of cover spread across the deck. Advance as fast as you can, but do not do anything stupid. Support each other in the advance, and make over-lapping fields of fire. They may only be slaver scum, but do not let that get you cocky. We move fast, hit them hard. Do not give them time to organize."

"We givin' any quarter?" Abdul asked. Saira looked towards Will for an answer to that. Will judged the faces looking at him, weighting his answer.

"I'm inclined not to give any quarter," he finally announced. "What do you all think?" A deep sound like the growl of a large animal answered him. While no saints themselves, Wind Dancer's crew wasn't much inclined to mercy towards slavers or raiders to begin with, and the tales of Hu Fan had only hardened that inclination. Will nodded at this response as if he expected no less.

"No quarter it is then," he proclaimed.

Everyone had their own reasons to hate slavers, Saira reflected. The older veterans had already chosen not to become wolves after the war, despite how easy it would be given the savagery around them. The younger crew had seen what true evil outlaws and reavers did, and rejected it. They may have joined for the money, or the killing, or both, but there some lines that were not crossed. The actions of Hu Fan at their last meeting had crossed those lines, she thought, and they all knew it. Dancers did not forget, or forgive.

"I want to remind you though," Will said, "what our primary mission is. What we're here for is a metal cylinder about so tall marked with a thunderbolt." He held his hands about two feet apart. "That's our pay off. I reckon that Hu Fan will either have that below decks in his quarters, or in a strong room somewhere. First to find it, let Saira or me know. If we're still fighting, we'll start to regroup to the lift point with it. That's our first priority. All goes well we'll lift with it, and burn the ship down." There was a second growl of agreement around the room at that. "Otherwise we keep at them until they're all dead, and then we find it." He looked around with his eyebrow raised, "any questions?"

"Do we care about the ship?" asked Tikku. She had two fighting sticks thrust through her belt besides pistols and she toted a shotgun almost as large as she was.

"Not as such," Will replied. "We're getting paid enough that we don't need her for a prize." He held up a finger in admonishment, "That said, no grenades, and the Hotchkisses will be slanting their fire. We want that cylinder; I don't want to sink the ship under us before we get it."

Georgios, as usual before a boarding rasped, "What we getting paid for this bloody cylinder again?"

Will grinned at him, and repeated the figure. There was a moment of almost reverent awe at the sum.

"Must be somebody's bloody nacker for that much," Georgios growled. Everyone laughed. Then the chime sounded overhead, signaling that they were nearing the attack run. Saira quickly ticked them off into two teams either to follow the Captain or her.

"Any problems, or final questions?" Saira asked. Silence answered her. She nodded as if that was what she had expected. "Alright," Saira said, "get to the bay, watch each other's back, and remember..." On cue everyone raised their fists and roared the Wind Dancer motto with one voice, "No one gets left behind!" Not a one of them, quick or dead, would be abandoned when the ship lifted as was common among some other airships. That mattered. That was what made them Wind Dancers. They moved quickly down the corridor towards the cargo doors. Every one of them, Saira thought with satisfaction, knew that Hu Fan was as good as dead.

# Chapter Seven

Foredeck, the Sea Ship Destiny

Indian Ocean

Yuan had served Hu Fan since the time when he was still a boy. When the Sky Demons had come, they had destroyed everything in Yuan's young world. His father's last act had been to push his son through a small gate in the compound wall before the Demons fire ray had taken him, obliterating both Yuan's family and his home in flame and terror.

He had become one of the many refugees, stripped of position and wealth. He was always hungry and scared. Hu Fan had found him, and promised that if Yuan followed him, he would never be scared again. Until recently, Hu Fan had kept that promise. Yuan had learned from his teacher well, becoming deadly and ruthless, while to Yuan's mind Hu Fan had become even more cunning over the years. They had preyed on the weak sheep of the whole South Seas, and everyone was afraid of them. They had prospered and their joss had grown. But now, Yuan was the one afraid.

It had started when his master, Hu Fan, had entered into the accursed deal with the pale Englishman who called himself Thaddeus Kane. Hu Fan agreed to smuggle the small cylinder, which seemed to have a great value for something so small. The addition of the woman Scholar that Kane had lured aboard with him at the last moment was a trivial matter in comparison. It was easier than a hold of human sheep to carry. Too easy for the money, Yuan now saw.

Of course, Hu Fan had no intention of honoring the deal. Once they were in the open seas, Hu Fan planned to be rid of Kane, and then negotiate better prices with whoever would pay most for either the cylinder or the woman Scholar. They had done such many times over the years. That was how the world worked.

But then, in Hu Fans cabin, the impossible had happened. The Englishman Kane had drunk the poisoned tea strong enough to kill a dozen men, with no effect save to rouse the Englishman's anger. The ensuing fight had been a nightmare. Kane had crushed the throats of two of Yuan's best men before they could even raise their swords. Kane had shrugged off both bullets and sword thrusts with ease, killing men with his bare hands until Yuan had taken him from behind. A single sword stroke had decapitated the monster. For monster Kane had been. No honest red blood that gushed came out of the trunk of the twitching body Yuan had severed the head from, only a pale pink jelly-like fluid that slowly oozed. For the first time in his life, Yuan had seen Hu Fan as terrified as he was himself.

They had calmed the crew after disposing of the body. Many whispered of devils and evil spirits angered. Yuan had beaten some of the whisperers himself while terrified that they were right. Hu Fan had not been himself ever since, taking to his cabin, singing strange prayers in the night. Then the accursed airship had found them.

Hu Fan had stayed in his cabin like a woman, leaving Yuan to rally the crew to fight off the Wind Dancer. Yuan remembered Hunting Owl from before as a cunning warrior. That he simply didn't stand off and use their cursed lightning cannon said that Hunting Owl wanted something other than revenge, likely either the cylinder or the woman. Hu Fan would have known how to use that knowledge to their advantage. Yuan simply didn't care. He had no intention of trying to bargain with Hunting Owl. That would show weakness. Even now he watched the blinking light from the airship pleading with him to surrender, which simply gave away how weak they were.

It also meant that Yuan had a chance. He had ordered them to turn about so that the fore cannon could be used to better effect. No air captain risked his ship getting holed lightly. If Yuan could keep the looming grey hulk beyond boarding range until dark, they might still slip away. Thus, he had come to the forecastle to take command of the main gun himself.

"No, you son of a sow," Yuan screamed. He kicked the gunner away from the sight. "The elevation must be higher!" he waved angrily at the two deck hands who frantically worked to raise the gun barrel.

Yuan placed himself to sight the barrel, and waved for them to stop. He grimaced while taking hold of the firing lanyard. "Now, die!" he screamed at the ship and jerked the lanyard. The gun gave a roar. Yuan followed the shot, seeing it fall just short of the lower hull of windows where he knew the ship was steered from.

The gun crew leaped forward to reload the gun, while Yuan watched the ship come closer. Suddenly, there was a flash that blinded him, followed by a roaring hiss like a thousand snakes. Yuan, still blinded, fell to the deck screaming, his skin afire.

The Wind Dancer had fired its lightning cannon in front of the Destiny's bow, causing not only those who were looking up to be blinded, but also creating a cloud of hot steam to explode over the fore deck, scalding the defenders as it passed. The airship glided forward, turning smoothly sideways as it came to rest over the deck gun. The Hotchkiss guns on the side of the Dancer opened fire, their rotating barrels firing heavy caliber rounds at a rate of thirty a minute, shredding both men and the wooden aft deck where the Gatling guns were mounted. From Dancer's open cargo bay, Will, Saira, and her Tigers slid down ropes to land on the raised foredeck of the sailing ship.

Crouching low as bullets sang overhead, Will started to low walk to the relative safety of the rear guardrail, when his ankle was grabbed by one of the still writhing gun crew. The blind man was screaming while clawing to reach a sword on his belt. Will quickly shot him once in the head for mercy. The hand jerked back, the screaming man going quiet as he died.

Reaching the railing for cover, Will looked left to see that the rest had gotten to similar refuge. The only thing that had let them get to cover was the Hotchkiss fire keeping most of the slavers heads down. He knew though that they couldn't wait here long, or the slavers could rally and charge, hoping to overwhelm them with numbers. Saira signaled to him that they needed to advance. He signaled back agreement.

With an ululating scream Saira sprang up, a green spark twinkling from the twin horned muzzle of her rifle as she fired, the dry crack of the bolt cleaving the air. Will saw one of her new Tigers, Ravin was his name Will recalled, spring up behind her, his automatic shotgun booming as he fired. A splash of light and smoke appeared on Ravin's chest, followed by the crack of a sparkie as he went down. Will cursed, peering ahead trying to see the shooter. Hu Fans men did have electrics.

Saira glanced behind her as the young man fell. Her head whipped back towards the rear of the ship, and then in rapid secession she fired off three bolts, the cracks loud as a giant's bull-whip, emerald muzzle flashes strobing as she gave that piercing undulating cry again. Saira then leapt over the railing with the rest of her team behind her, all of them taking up her scream like a war cry. She ducked down again as the others fanned out behind her, popped up to fire again, then sought cover behind the crates and bales lashed to the deck.

Will signaled to his group, while drawing his Bowie in his other hand. Screaming his own war cry, he sprang over the side, the others of his group yelling and firing as they came behind him. He almost landed on a slaver who had trying to been sneaking up under the railing. His knife slashed down at a face that reflected the same surprise that Will felt. As the slaver fell, Will flinched at the whistle of a bullet passing near his head. Snarling. his gun punched a hole in a rifleman's chest across the deck from him. Then he dove for the cover of a crate.

What followed was a whirling hell of shooting, stabbing, punching, and ducking, as the Dancers made their way across the deck of the ship, pushing the desperate slavers back into the maw of the Hotchkiss guns field of fire. Will paused behind a bail to reload. Shoving his knife point down into the deck beside him, he broke open the breach of his revolver, feeding shells into the barrel by feel instead of sight, all the while scanning the battle with his eyes.

They'd come more than two thirds of the way down ship. The slavers appeared vastly outgunned. There wasn't any more electric fire from their side and it seemed that they had no suits to protect from the deadly bolts. The Hotchkiss guns roaring fire overhead was preventing any of the slavers from reaching the aft deck with its Gatling guns, mostly the Dancers were being met with blades and gunpowder pistols now.

Will knew their advantage was about to change as his people's sparkies ran out of charge. He saw Saira across from him, disemboweling an ax wielder with her twin blades. Fortunately, there didn't seem to be any coordination to the defense, which puzzled Will. He knew that Hu Fan was a clever fighter, but his men seemed both confused and demoralized. He saw another slaver turn to run, when a bolt caught the man. He fell, spinning and twitching, dead before he hit the deck. Will still hadn't seen Hu Fan among the defenders. What was the old bastard planning, he worried watching for some trick of the old slaver.

The main resistance left seemed to be a small group that had pulled some barrels and bails into a barricade before a pair of ordinate doors leading into the underside of the aft deck. The Hotchkiss had slowed to sporadic firing, wary of hitting the approaching Dancers.

Will cocked his revolver, and leaned over the top of the bail. He fired quickly, the barrels turning as fast as he could pull the trigger. Three of the slavers behind the makeshift barricade fell as if pole axed, the others flinched down. In that moment, Saira and Tikku sprinted across the deck, vaulting the barricade. Saira with her long knives whirling like buzz saws and Tikku with her fighting sticks in each hand. The two turned the defenders into a knot of confusion, slicing throats and crushing skulls.

Cursing all damn fools, Will pulled up his Bowie knife and leapt around the bail he'd been behind. Yelling, he charged forward shooting as he went. His last shot caught a sallow faced man who had been about to shoot Saira in the back. He jumped the barricade swinging, empty gun in one hand, knife in the other. The three were joined by other Dancers, swarming in with long knives and deadly intent. In seconds, they were the only ones still standing before the doors. Will looked at Saira, as they stood among the carnage, breath heaving.

"That was just a mite crazy, you know." Hunting Owl remarked to her. Saira laughed, flicking blood off the long blades in her hands. She was covered in crimson, none of which Will assumed was hers.

"Not really Cap'n Will," Saira smiled at him. "You had spooked them right well with your shooting. Tikku and I just thought we would just take advantage of the moment." Will laughed back, as the other sounds of battle began falling silent.

"Well, looks as if you were right." Will allowed. He looked around in the suddenly eerie silence that can sometimes occur at the end of a fight. "Appears we got this one," He observed unnecessarily. Saira nodded, raising her voice to for a check.

"Everyone, sound off," the Arms-Master trumpeted. They both listened as every one of the Tigers shouted their name and how they were. Will was relieved that barring a few wounds, they hadn't lost anyone. Saira also breathed easier when the last voice called out. She smiled at Will.

"Well, no batch of low life slaver scum is better than we are any day, yes?" She clicked her knives together for emphasis. Will made a sound of agreement.

"Don't get too happy yet," he warned. "We still need that cylinder. Did you see anything of Hu Fan?" Saira shook her head, then pointed with a knife towards the doors.

"Do you figure he is in there?" she wondered. Will nodded as he sheathed his Bowie knife.

"That's what I reckon," he said. "I want you to take over here and look for a cargo hold." He reloaded his revolver again, checked the load, and then closed the gun with a snap. "I think I'll pay our host a visit in his cabin, give him our best wishes," he finished with a grim grin.

"Let me come with you," Saira asked simply. Will shook his head.

"No. I can do this one fine," he said. "Secure the ship, search for that cylinder. I'll be back with you before you know it." He flashed her his boyish grin. She started to say something, and then merely gave him her sharp nod.

"As you say, Cap'n," Saira said. She returned his grin with one of her own. "Be safe alright?"

"Of course," he returned. Crossing to the doors, he looked them over for some sort of trap or trigger. With a shrug he worked the handle, discovering that the door wasn't even bolted, and with a quick look back at Saira and Tikku, he hefted his revolver and slid into the dark.

Saira struggled with her urge to follow him. She knew they were not clear of danger yet, her spirit sense told her so. Instead, she looked back down the length of the ship. Dead bodies littered the deck, thankfully none of them Dancers. She wanted to pause to sing offerings of glory and the dead to the Serpent Mother, but did not. She had learned that some of the crew grew uneasy when she did that, for some reason, besides there was still more to do, especially if there was still more danger.

"Listen up you Tigers!" As the others raised their heads again she began called out orders. "Tommy! Georgios! Tether the Dancer to the fore deck. Anyone wounded get back topside and seen to! Ravin! Tikku! On me!" When the younger man shuffled over to her, she looked him over skeptically.

"Go topside and report to Mr. Rogers, she ordered. "Say to him exactly this: 'Ship taken. Cap'n gone in search of the fat rat, still searching for packet,' then report to Dr. Wu to look at you."

"I am fine Master Saira," Ravin protested." Let me stay here and help." Saira's face turned stern.

"That was an order, Mr. Singh, the Arms-Master said. "It would be best if you followed it. You took a full on jolt there. I warned you to button it up tight! You are fortunate to still be alive." She slapped him on the shoulder, and continued in a gentler voice, "You did fine today Ravin, just fine. Go take the bunk time while you can. Now repeat back the message. He did so. She nodded when he was finished, slightly less concerned that the jolt may have affected his reason. She had seen it happen.

"Good," she replied, "Now go. We will discuss the proper sealing of your suit another time." She watched as the young man make his way carefully across the deck. She had seen sparkie injuries appear from nowhere before, the jerking limbs, the scattered thinking. She felt that he would likely be alright. Tikku shook her head standing beside her.

"Men," the other woman sighed. "Why do they always have to be so difficult?" Saira looked at her sideways.

"Because they think that if they do stupid strutting things, they have more chance of getting in our yoni," Saira remarked dryly. They both laughed. Tikku's eyes followed the young mans' back as he walked towards the lift ropes.

"Well, I think that he has a good chance as it is," Tikku observed. Saira looked at her in surprise, then slapped the other woman's arm in friendly encouragement with a grin. They both laughed again. Tikku pointed to Saira's bracer.

"Could you not have called the message in on that instead of having Ravin deliver it?" Saira looked down at her arm and shrugged.

"Perhaps," she replied. "To be honest I forgot it was there. Besides, Ravin needed something to get him upstairs, and this way I know that Rogers will get the message."

Saira looked around one more time to see that everyone was moving about their jobs, checking that the wounded slavers were really dead, taking up positions to guard the deck. They were good devils, the lot of them. She felt the combination of tiredness and exaltation she always felt after battle, but there was no time for that. The sooner they were off this ship, the better. She knew trouble was still here.

"Come on," she said to Tikku, "Let us go searching for this tiny treasure."

Will cat footed down the dark narrow hall. He'd met no one so far, but he could smell the rich scent of joss sticks burning ahead of him. Light leaked from the cracks around the door at the end of the hall, which he figured was where his quarry hid. He kicked at the door. It sprang open with surprising ease. He slid into the room and stopped.

Hu Fan sat on a throne like chair, wrapped in a silk shroud, unmoving. His gaze was fixed on two boxes resting on the teak table before him, his hands lightly resting on their plungers. The boxes had wires that led off into the walls of the room. Will stopped cold at the sight of them, even while his gun barrels on Hu Fan.

"William Hunting Owl," Hu Fan croaked without looking up. "I had thought that you would come for me yourself."

"It's all over Hu Fan." Will said quietly, "Give me the cylinder you took on, and you might still get out of this."

The old man began laughing softly, "The cylinder is meaningless now. Of course it is over. It was over the moment I trafficked with demons and devils. I have done many things, but never have I cursed my soul and had my luck desert me so."

Will had no idea what he was on about. Slowly he moved forward, gun steady.

"That's as may be, Hu Fan. But I can still end your scummy life right now, you know. You don't have any tortured women to hide behind this time."

Hu Fan laughed harder, so hard that his shoulders rocked.

"Ah, William Hunting Owl, you will thank me for saving you, you know. The only safety we all have now is death!" He looked up at Will, his eyes blazing with madness. "The Demons are coming, and it is best we die now!" Will shot him through the head while he talked.

Hu Fan jerked back with the force of the bullet; one hand pushed down on a plunger, while the other fell away. There came a muffled whoop as the ship rocked. There was the sudden smell of burning wood. The crazy bastard had fired the ship!

Will quickly looked around the cabin, seeing a small fortune in the furnishings. He spotted a large key on the table next to the plungers, and scooped it up. Running back up the hallway, he burst out on to the deck, amid the exclamations of his crew. Turning he saw the thick smoke that billowed from the far aft.

"He's fired the ship," Will yelled, while waving his arms. "Start moving towards the lift!"

Saira came up out of the hold with Tikku behind her.

"Cap'n!" She shouted. "We've found the strong room! We cannot open it though."

Will held up the key, "Where is it?" he shouted. Pointing the way, Saira led the three of them down the ramp to a large door with thick iron bands and a strong lock.

Will shoved the key into the lock. It turned, with a click. They pulled open the heavy door, and stopped in amazement.

Inside stood a white woman with red hair, dressed as a European toff. She stood up straight and looked at them without fear, a length of chain ready at her side.

"I," she announced, "am Lady Abigail Hadley, Royal Scholar of the British Empire. If you aid in my release, I am sure that you may be rewarded."

Will took in the bucket in the corner, the unkempt state of her dress, and figured she was a captive. He swore to himself in as many languages as he knew. Was she going to go hysterical on him? The last thing he needed was to have to mollycoddle some Brit aristo. Hadley? Was she who the damned Scholar had been riling up the Spider? He noticed a Scholar's badge on the lapel of her jacket. He bowed sardonically, his revolver waving to one side.

"Well, Lady Abigail Hadley, of the British Empire," he said to her, "if you'll kindly step out of that strong room so we can loot it, I'm sure we can oblige you somehow. But if you don't drop that chain, we can always just shoot you now." Saira and Tikku shared a glance, their eyes rolling at

Will's speech. They both knew he would never do any such thing to any prisoner of Hu Fan's. The aristocratic woman's shoulders slumped. She slowly dropped the chain she had been holding, and came towards them on unsteady legs. Will held out a one hand offering to steady her, the other pointing his gun at her.

"It's alright," he said in what he hoped was a more soothing tone. He really didn't have time for this. The ship lurched. Lady Hadley grabbed a hold of the door frame to steady herself at the same moment that Will did. "I promise that neither me nor mine will harm you," He continued as patiently as he could, "but we really need to move right quickly here. The ship's on fire you see." With a startled look, the woman came out more quickly, ignoring Wills hand. He waved towards Saira. "Saira, take her top side to my day cabin. See that she's alright, and stay with her." He raised his eyebrow in silent order.

Saira nodded at Will in understanding. If the woman was playing some kind of deep game, Saira might be able to ferret it out with her powers. If she was a victim, and had been brutalized, she was the best person on board to help her. She took the Englishwoman gently by the arm.

"Come on now," she said as gently as she could, let's get you out of here." She held out a hand towards her which again Abigail shrugged off. The Englishwoman turned back to Will.

"There was an Englishman named Thaddeus Kane aboard, Is he among you?" Will raised an eyebrow in surprise.

"Sorry to say, we found no Englishmen." He went on more softly, hoping she wouldn't faint or something. "Chances are Hu Fan killed him already." Her eyes lit with a fire that Will hadn't expected to see.

"Good. Then I won't have to kill him myself." She turned to Saira, "lead the way, thank you."

Will watched them ascend the ramp. Another bloody aristo savant named Hadley? Not too damn likely. Well, he thought, one thing at a time. He turned back to the contents of the room and pointed.

"That one Tikku! Handle it gently like over to me."

~~~

Abigail stood blinking in the sunlight. The woman next to her was a touch shorter than herself. She had very short black hair and was clearly some sort of Hindu half-caste. She wore the same black suit as the others, with a rifle slung across her back, two very long knives at her belt and a pair of goggles shoved up on her forehead. To Abigail's amazement, she began undoing the frogs of her tunic, showing a very ample, and very bare, bosom. The woman took a deep breath, and sighed.

"Ah, fresh air is good."

Abigail took a breath herself, and nearly choked. The air held an almost impossible stench, doubtless caused by the many dead bodies that littered the deck and the black ominous smoke billowing from the rear of the ship, which did indeed appear to be on fire. Whoever her saviors were, they were deadly people indeed. She looked up, and saw the bulk of an airship overhead. There were lines of rope leading from the deck up into the dark maw of the ship. As she watched, a man holding onto one was pulled quickly up into its depths.

"This way Lady Hadley," the woman gestured them towards the ropes. "My name is Saira by the way, Saira Brighton." She gently extended her kalas, sensing the innocent wariness of an animal feeling trapped. "I hope things haven't been too bad for you," she said, looking at the British woman carefully. "We do have healing means on board if you need them." Her voice, Abigail judged, held only genuine concern as she took her double meaning. She shook her head at the woman.

"No thank you, Saira. Did I get that right?" She pronounced it Sigh-ra as she thought she had heard it. Saira nodded at her, continuing to weave her spirit magic on the unsuspecting woman. The intent was only to get her to feel relaxed with Saira, and so required a more subtle mind touch than something such as she had used on Smeadly.

"I mean to say while there were bad things," Abigail continued, "there was no bad in that sense." Her face grimaced. "Fortunate I suppose, although I was left with the sense that it was more of the 'don't bruise the fruit, so we can't sell it,' than any good fortune. Horrible feeling in its own way," She shook her head, as if to clear it. "I do beg your pardon for going on." She stopped, looking at the woman, and tried on a smile. With the ship on fire, she judged she had no choice but to go along with these people if they would have her. Doubtless the waters were full of sharks. At least they acted more politely than her last captors. "Please call me Abigail, Lady Hadley was my mother." Saira smiled at this.

"Right then, Abigail," Saira said. "We will get you up topside, and have a nice cup of tea. You are not afraid of heights I hope?" They had reached the ropes. Abigail looked up and swallowed. It looked a long ways up.

"No, not as such," she said. "Although, I am afraid though that I am not familiar with this means of transport." The woman, Saira, grabbed a rope and was attaching a hook to a ring on her belt. She then placed one foot into a stirrup, and held out her arms towards Abigail.

"Oh, that is as no mind, really," Saira said reassuringly, "All you have to do is place your foot on top of mine and wrap your arms around me very tight." Abigail attempted to follow these instructions only to have the woman pull her even tighter to her. Beneath the sweat, Saira, smelled of spice and incense. Abigail hated to think what she must smell like given the privations of her voyage, although Saira did not seem bothered by it. While Abigail had appreciated the charms of her own sex in the past, she found her current thoughts puzzling at best. It must be a form of shock she decided. After all, it wasn't every day one went from being kidnapped by pirates only to being rescued by other pirates.

"There we are, Abigail," Saira said softly to her. Realizing that she was about to be pulled some hundreds of feet up into the air, she pulled the Hindu woman even closer and swallowed.

"Saira," she asked in a small voice, "does anyone ever fall off?"

"Not while I hold them," Saira reassured her. Before Abigail could think better of it, Saira suddenly pulled on the rope. They were hurled upwards at an incredible speed before Abigail could catch her breath. Saira deftly swung the two of them over and onto the deck of the hold, Abigail still clinging to her tightly. Saira laughed.

"You can let go now, Abigail," she assured the woman. "It's safe." Abigail disentangled herself quickly, looking first at the other woman, then down at the ship far below. She swallowed, seeking to steady her breathing.

"Well," Abigail said blandly, I must say that now I have literally been swept off my feet." Saira's face was a momentary study in surprise. Then she laughed out loud, as did the others in the bay who heard Abigail's remark.

"You are a bit alright, Abigail," Saira proclaimed as she unhooked her belt, She shook the line free, and draped it back over the open hatch. Abigail watch as the line was lowered again, and then looked up attempting to discern the mechanism.

"Electric pulleys, very efficient, "she nodded approvingly.

"Well," Saira said with a shrug, "They do the job. Come on," she smiled at Abigail, "tea is this way."

# Chapter Eight

Wind Dancer, over the Indian Ocean

Saira watched the woman eat another bowl of the soup that was always available in the mess. She sat across from her in Cap'n Will's day cabin, inclined to think that Lady Hadley was who she said she was. Clearly she hadn't eaten much for some time, yet still ate with manners suited for a toff dinner party. Hard to play act that. As Abigail daintily finished, Saira pushed the tea mug across the table to her.

"There, feeling somewhat better?" She asked with true sympathy. Saira had known hunger and the fear of captivity herself at one time.

"Yes, thank you," Abigail replied. "I can't say when I've eaten a more delicious soup." Abigail picked up the mug with now steady hands. She looked around the cabin. Everything she had seen so far was clean and very tidy, even the corridors. That didn't mean anything of course. Perhaps they were simply tidy bloodthirsty killers.

The cabin itself seemed an eclectic mix of souvenirs from far off places. Little statues of strange gods stood over a pigeon holed section of wall that doubtless held maps, next to a bookcase full of old volumes. The chairs were of a light cane weave, quite comfortable, although oddly enough bolted in place on the floor.

Abigail thought to herself, if she could get the other woman talking, maybe she could better ascertain her situation. That the crew of the ship were capable of violence was clear. Who were they? What did they intend with her?

"I hadn't realized that an airship like this would have so much room inside it," Abagail remarked. Saira sipped her own tea, all the while extending her senses to read the woman's aura for signs of any deception. She was becoming more deeply in rapport.

"Well," she said, "the Dancer is plenty roomy, not as roomy as a merchant ship, where people have their families, or a dreadnought where there's a mile or more of space. Story is that she was originally some warlord's toy, more ground support frigate than cruiser really, for all that she is as big as one. She carries no heavy broadsides you see?" here Saira smiled evilly. "That has led more than one raider to underestimate us."

"I see," Abigail remarked. The other woman looked to be about her age, yet she spoke much as she had heard the old veterans talking in the pubs. "You sound as if you know ships well. What exactly do you do aboard, if I may ask? I assume that you don't fight all the time."

"Of course, you may ask, I'm the ships Arms-Master." Saira smiled at her, feeling their auras touching. A few more sentences and she would be attuned enough to know if the Englishwoman lied when she spoke, without the Brit ever being aware of Saira's ability.

"I'm sorry," Abigail frowned, "but I'm afraid I don't know what that means."

"It means that I am the chief fighter, so, yes, I 'fight all the time' as you say." Seeing Abigail's surprise, Saira laughed. "I lead those who go on boarding raids such as we did today, as well as oversee those who man the ship's weapons. I also train everyone in how to fight should it be needed. Not everyone aboard drops down the hatch, but they all need to be good fighters. "

"I see," Abigail said wonderingly. "How did you come by such a profession?" She had met a few women Army and Navy officers before, but this small woman was nothing like them.

Saira shrugged in such a way that Abigail was momentarily reminded that beneath the open rubber tunic, the woman was practically half naked. Confound it, she needed to focus on what she said next, not ogle like a schoolboy.

"My mother's people are all warriors." Saira was aware of the Englishwoman being aware of her. When auras touched, body spoke to body even when one of them did not know what was happening. "I learned much there. My father's brother taught me more," she explained. "He took over one of the great cargo ships at the end of the war as a merchant. I lived aboard her for a time. When I went my own way, I found the Dancer. She's a good ship. Will Hunting Owl is the best Captain I have ever seen."

"I see," Abigail said. She took another sip of tea. The woman certainly had a...presence for lack of a better word. Still her voice rang true. She'd heard of the Alliance of Nations giving freighter ships to crews after the war as a way to stimulate world trade as part of the Reconstruction. The planet had been so devastated by the Invaders that anything that would help the survivors was done. Back home at Oxford, they still ate fruit and vegetables grown in Spain and North Africa. There simply wasn't enough un-blighted land around. These and other products were delivered by the giant air freighters. However, this ship was clearly no freighter. She startled as a chime sounded the overhead speaker. A woman's bright voice spoke cryptic instructions in a British boarding school accent.

"That will be the signal that we are getting underway," Saira explained.

"Forgive me, while I am grateful for you removing me from that horrid situation, I must ask." Abigail wet her lips. "Are you pirates? More to the point, what are your intentions towards me?" Saira sensed the woman's fear being controlled by a strong determination to not be controlled by another. She eyed her with a new respect. This was no fainting lady, for all that she was British.

"Truly, we are not pirates," Saira answered her seriously. "I forgive you that you do not know what an insult your question is, though you would not be the first to make it. No, we are a Free Airship," she said with pride.

"It means that we are beholden to no one," Saira continued, seeing Abigail's incomprehension. "We are flagged out of the Freeport of Seattle, on the other side of the Pacific. Many free airships are merchants; some are like us, armed fighters. We do jobs that armed ships do. We run small special cargoes, guard unarmed ships, patrol the smaller trade routes where there's trouble and such. The jobs your big shiny air navies can't be bothered with. We do have warrants to hunt and kill pirates where we find them." Saira's smile now held nothing of its earlier merriment. And we do kill them. Like today."

"So then, you are, ah, privateers?" Abigail asked interested, despite the blood-thirsty sentiment. She knew that the Freeports were one of the more controversial provisions of the Gibraltar Treaty. The idea had been to create air and sea ports around the world that would be international territory with no taxes or restrictions. The notion had been that they would also stimulate world trade. What they turned out to be, in practice, was quite different. Most of Mrs. McDougal's more lurid serials took place in Freeports. Mrs. M had been Abigail's nanny and the Hadley's housekeeper since Abigail was quite young. Right then Abigail missed her something fierce.

"I have heard that term used by some," Saira allowed. "We fight when we must or when we are paid to." Saira smiled again, "And we are very well paid. We are answerable to the Freeport council where we are flagged. Pirates steal what they want, kill who they want, and enslave the rest for money. We are not like that!" Saira said forcefully.

"As for our intentions, that is up to Cap'n Will," Saira continued. "I can promise you that none aboard will touch you with lascivious intention without you wanting them to, and that we will get you somewhere more or less safe." She looked at Abigail, listening with more than her ears. "Now then, how is it that a Lady such as you came to be in such a way?"

"Actually," Will said from the doorway, "I was going to ask the same thing." He walked in to the cabin with steaming mug, and sat down behind the battered desk. The man grinned at her broadly, then placed his feet up on the desk, boots and all. Abigail found this familiarity very disconcerting. He looked from one woman to the next "Please go on, Lady Hadley."

Abigail found that she was flustered again by his regard, which was most out of character for her. This Captain Hunting Owl had a strong presence of his own. Certainly there was an animal sensuality about him mixed with a sense of danger. But there was more than that. There was such an air of authority that you simply had to pay attention to him when he entered a room. She wondered what the protocol was here. She didn't see Saira standing when he entered, as she'd seen the crew do when the captain had entered a room on her air flight from Britain. Then there was this Captain's casual familiarity. While she dithered over what was the correct thing to say, she sipped her tea. The silence lengthened. Finally, Will appeared to take pity on her.

"Suppose I start," he said, still sounding very genial. "Do you know where your servants are?"

"Actually there aren't any servants." Abigail took a breath. "I am traveling on my own." She hesitated, knowing now how foolish she had been, and how she would sound. Will raised an eyebrow at that, but made no remark. He nodded at her to go on.

"Well, "Abigail said somewhat defensively, "Really, it should not matter that I am a woman traveling alone should it? It is the 1890's after all. You see, I was on my way to meet with my father who is engaged in research in China. We are, in fact, to meet in Hong Kong."

"Pardon me," Will asked around his mug. "Who is your father exactly?"

"Lord Robert Hadley, also of the Royal Order of Scholars," She replied. "He contacted me to join him, as I believe I mentioned." Abigail's hands clutched tightly to her tea mug. "In the course of my travels, I met what I thought at the time was a British gentleman named Thaddeus Kane. I learned that he certainly was not one. Mr. Kane offered to succor me on the last of my journey from Bombay to Hong Kong by offering me passage on what he claimed was one of his ships."

"This Kane said he was a shipper, and you were in luck as he had a ship sailing that night." Will said dryly. "Once you were on board, he offered you something to drink. When you woke up, you found that you were not just a guest." Abigail looked at him in wonder.

"Yes, that is exactly what happened! How did you know?" She demanded.

"He didn't," said Saira gently, "It is an old slavers trick. What they call a 'Shanghai'."

"Yes!" Abigail exclaimed, "The large Chinese man said something like that when I awoke."

"That would be Hu Fan?" Will asked.

"Yes, that was his name," Abigail said, visibly suppressing a shudder. "He told me that he was the captain of the ship, and I had been 'shanghaied.'"

"So, how is it that you came to be in the strong room?" Will wondered, "Seems a funny place to put you." Abigail knew that she was blushing now, and cursed inwardly. Her fair skin did that to her every time.

"Well, I'm afraid that I have something of a temper at times," she explained, keeping her eyes on the wall behind Saira. "When he said that I was a captive, and leered over me, I'm afraid that I attacked him, and," here she paused to drink her tea. "I, ahem, bit off part of his, his ear," she said hesitantly.

Both Saira and Will went very still at this surprising revelation. Then Saira began what Abigail thought was a mostly girlish giggling, which seemed very out of place given her martial attire. She was still even covered in splashes of blood. Saira was now laughing so hard, she was gasping.

"Oh Shiva!" she exclaimed between whoops, "You'd best be careful, Cap'n, she has a temper!"

"I am sorry," Abigail said coldly, "I fail to see what is remotely amusing about this."

"Lady Hadley," Will begin slowly. "Hu Fan was a vicious cold killer and a slaver. The last time we tangled, he threatened to flay a woman alive just to keep us at a distance from him. He later began to shove his cargo, which was living men, women, and children overboard just so he could have his ship go faster." Abigail's face went from red to ghostly pale as the implications began to sink in.

"My god," she whispered.

"Aiya," Will nodded." So far as I know, you're the only person I've heard of to do Hu Fan bodily harm and live to tell of it." He grinned at her like a boy, then drained his mug.

"Well, second person now," he said with a satisfied air. "After I put a bullet through his head."

"Too good for him, Cap'n," Saira said intensely, still wiping her eyes from laughing.

"Well, I was a might rushed you could say," Will explained. He turned back to Abigail "So, Lady Hadley, you are a very lucky woman, I'm thinking." He put down his mug on the desk, uncurling his legs to have his feet hit the floor.

"So, what are you a Scholar of?" he asked. "Don't you types all have areas that you specialize in?"

"Please, call me Abigail, Captain, as I do owe you a debt of gratitude." She requested, coming to a quick decision. She may as well try to make allies here. At least, they seemed like friendly people, if not exactly civilized. "Titles are given to most anyone who can do their sums these days," she explained easily, "As you know, when Her Majesty created the Order of Scholars after the War, it was designed not only to be a bulwark of the New Science against the return of the Invaders but to be a revival of the British aristocracy." She waved a hand gracefully. "Most who graduate from Oxford become titled these days. As to my studies, they lie in the areas of Electric Energetics, both theoretical and applied."

"You mean like what makes Tesla engines run and such?" Saira asked innocently. Tesla's inventions had not only contributed to the salvation of humanity from the Invaders, but formed the cornerstone of much of the modern world. Abigail smiled at her.

"Precisely!" She exclaimed. "Although more towards the 'and such' of those studies. There is so much just in this field that is wonderful," she stopped herself from continuing with an effort, and returned her hands to her lap. "But I do not mean to allow my enthusiasms to run away there." She said. Lady Hadley turned back to Will.

"I truly do have to reach Hong Kong though, Captain," Abigail said. "I cannot offer you much in the way of remuneration immediately, but I do promise that I shall see you compensated. That is, if you can get me to somewhere that I might continue on my way easily." Will glanced at Saira. The Arms-Master turned both hands palm up, their secret signal that Saira thought they were telling only the truth.

"I think that she is good Cap'n," Saira said. "Hells, after that story about Hu Fan, I would lend her my underwear!"

Will nodded in decision. He'd never known Saira to be wrong yet about someone she was reading. Still, there was her father's poking around in Hong Kong to consider. Maybe the daughter showing up would distract the old man from whatever he was doing in the Asian underground. It never hurt to have another aristocrat think well of you. He looked at Abigail and grinned again.

"Well, Lady...Abigail," he caught himself, remembering her wishes about how she wanted to be addressed. "It seems that you really are on the good side of some spirits somewhere. So happens that we've got a cargo that we have to deliver to Hong Kong right quickly. Dancer may not be what you're used to, but we can have you in Hong Kong in seven or eight days if you're of a mind." He grinned his most boyish grin at her, "and for telling that story about Hu Fan, there'll be no charge either."

Abigail breathed a sigh of relief. She could see no reason for him to lie to her. After all, if his intentions were bad, there was very little she could do to stop him. Besides she didn't feel that Saira would support such intentions. There was something about Saira that gave Abigail the impression that Abigail knew her character well, even on such short acquaintance. She smiled back at him.

"Thank you, Captain," she replied. "I assure you that your accommodations will most certainly be superior to what I have experienced of late." Will and Saira smiled at this, as the light tube overhead chose that moment to flicker. At the same moment, the Bridge talker Naomi's voice sounded through the grill set in Wills desk summoning Will to the engine room.

"Sounds like I'd best go see what Devi has to say," Will stood up quickly and began moving towards the doorway.

"If you are having Tesla problems, Captain, it is possible that I may be able to assist. It is my area of specialty as you say." Abigail pointed out mildly. Will turned and looked at her.

"Well, that's right kind of you, Abigail," Will said mildly. "But Devi is as good as they come. She's kept this crate in the air for years now." He then turned to Saira, "You willing to take her on?" Saira looked at Abigail then back at Will.

"Sure, Cap'n," She said easily. "I got her." Will nodded.

"Put her in the cabin next to yours then," Will ordered. "Anyone have a problem, they can talk to me about it. Can you parcel out your duties for a couple of days while our guest gets settled in?"

Saira considered for a moment. "I still want to run the after action review. Besides that though, Tikku can run the drills, and Sebastian can see to post-action maintenance to the ship's guns." Will nodded in agreement.

"I'll let Rogers know for the roster, then," he said decisively. "Consider yourself off standard for a bit."

"Aiya, Cap'n Will," Saira grinned. She was sure the Englishwoman was no threat, but wouldn't argue the point, even if she wasn't sitting across from her. "Can I draw double rum rations? Have to entertain her and all that." Will shook his head in mock sorrow at his Arms-Master's sally. He turned to Abigail. "Watch yourself with this one, Lady Hadley. She is a sorceress of no small ability, and will catch you out with her charms."

"Like you, Cap'n?" Saira teased.

"I am a warrior of Wovoka, and immune to your wiles," he shot back with a grin, "and the answer to your request is no," he said firmly. "Lady Hadley can draw the same ration as everyone else, without any help." He looked up, as the light tube flickered again. He gave them both a little courtly bow that somehow didn't seem out of place to Abigail.

"Abigail, I'll leave you with Saira now, who really will see you safe and settled. I will talk to you both later."

"Thank you, Captain," Abigail began to say, only to see Will already moving out the doorway.

"You only think so, Cap'n! " Saira called to his back, and laughed as he made a warding gesture with his hand over his shoulder at her. Abigail blinked at Saira's comments.

"Are you always so...informal?" she asked the Arms-Master. Saira rose from the cabin chair where she was sitting. Abigail rose and followed her as they moved towards the doorway.

"You almost sound like Mr. Rogers, our First Officer," Saira looked at her smiling. "He's British too, says that I lack 'proper decorum'." She struck a much exaggerated pose with her nose in the air that almost made Abigail laugh out loud. Saira then dropped the pose, and waved her hands dismissively. "We do not generally bother with a lot of that 'yes sir, may I scratch myself sir' sort of thing on Dancer," she said. "Oh a bit, but only when it matters though. We have not offended you already have we?" Saira paused to look at her. Abigail smiled back at her as they stood by the door.

"Actually, I must say that I find it rather refreshing," Abigail replied. "I have little patience for that sort of thing myself."

"Well, we will do our best to refresh the hell out of you then, Abigail." Saira grinned at her. Her hand rested on the door handle. "Shall we get you settled in then? We will have to be quiet and quick passing through the bridge, but it is the easiest path to your berth." Abigail nodded for her to continue.

"Lead on," Abigail said with a nod. Saira opened the door. Together the two tip-toed across the bridge, keeping to one wall. Mr. Rogers regarded them for a moment from his station near the map table, then turned back to what he was doing without speaking to them. Once beyond the large steel doors that separated the bridge from the main corridor, Saira turned to Abigail and spoke softly.

"That was the bridge, where the ship is run from," she explained. "Never enter the bridge, the engine room, or the armory without permission. It is very much not allowed, unless you have business there." Abigail nodded at this solemnly. Saira smiled at the Scholar.

"It is not as if you will have anything to do with the running of the ship." She paused. After we get you settled, perhaps you might want to take a bath?" Abigail's eyes went wide at this offer, as she followed the dark skinned woman down the corridor. The few people she passed flattened themselves against the wall. Abigail caught flashes of annoyance on some of the faces, but taking her cue from Saira, ignored them.

"You have the means for a bath?" She inquired in amazement. Saira nodded.

"Actually," the Arms-Master replied, "we have a common bath with both hot and cold tubs sunk into the floor. It is part of the ballast system. I told you this used to be some warlords toy, yes? Well, apparently, he felt it important for his crew to be clean. Cap'n is the same way. One of the things he's insistent on actually." Saira gave her a sideways glance. "Course when I say 'common' I mean that we all share it together at the same time, boys and girls alike."

Abigail had read of such things being done before, but despite her view of herself as a modern enlightened woman, the idea was...unsettling. She had shared such activities only with a couple of very daring lovers. To cover her adjustment to the idea, she looked at around the corridor they were traveling. The walls were panels of a dark wood, the floor much the same, along the corners of the ceiling ran long light tubes that bathed the corridor in bright light. Her noise caught the faint scent of some spice in the air.

What caught her eye were the intricate carvings that ran along the join between floor and wall, wall and ceiling. Occasionally a whole wall panel had been carved into a scene. Though no artist, she could recognize that they were done with great skill. One of a small leaping deer that repeated down along the corridor seemed very lifelike.

"What incredible carvings," Abigail said, pointing. "They are beautiful."

"Yes, they are," Saira said indifferently. "Some of the crew whittle in their free time." The light tube above their heads dimmed to near darkness and after a long pause, brightened again.

"Vishnu's balls," Saira breathed, looking up.

"I take it this does not happen often?" Abigail asked. Saira shook her head.

"Never," the other woman said. Abigail stopped suddenly in the corridor, placing her hands on her hips.

"Take me to your engine room," she said abruptly in a tone that was not used to being argued with. She was after all a British Aristocrat and it was time she acted like one. Saira stopped with her, then mirrored Abigail by putting her hands on her hips as well. She frowned at the Scholar.

"Abigail, I do not think that is a really good idea," Saira said slowly. "Devi, our engineer, does not like outsiders there. Hell, she does not like most crew in her engine room." Abigail was clearly not to be moved.

"I believe I understand," she said implacably. "I do not enjoy others in my laboratory. But it appears something is occurring with the Tesla Engines, and this whole ship could be in danger." She changed her tone, raising a hand in supplication, "Truly, Saira, this is what I have spent my whole life in the study of, please let me help."

Saira had opened her spirit such she was aware that not only was the English woman speaking what she felt to be true, but that this was a moment where destinies converged. It wasn't often that she felt destiny tapping her on the shoulder, but this was one of them. The Spirits were saying that the Englishwoman was right. When the Spirits spoke it was as well that she listened. This was also likely going to get her in a lot of trouble with any number of people though. She sighed.

"Alright," she said wearily. "But you get to deal with Devi wanting to have us beheaded." She looked down at Abigail's skirts and bustle, then back up to her face. "Can you even climb a ladder in all that?" Lady Hadley straightened up.

"I can go where ever you lead," Abigail replied stoutly. Saira tried very hard not to let her skepticism show.

"Alright then," she pointed ahead. "We go down the ladder off to the left."

Saira opened a hatch set in the floor in a small alcove just off the corridor. She yelled down it her voice sounding as if it were going down a well.

"Ware! She shouted, "Red! I say again. Red Pass!" She looked up at Abigail. "If you ever hear someone shout that move out of their way quickly. It means that they are moving in an emergency to save the ship." She gestured down the hatchway. "Follow me, and keep up." The Arms-Master went down the ladder like grease. Abigail swallowed, and gathered her skirts to follow. She had difficulty getting the folds through the narrow opening but persevered. It wouldn't do to show her private person to everyone as they went by, she thought to herself.

"Are you coming?" Saira's voice drifted up impatiently.

When they finally entered the engine ready room, the discordant bone deep hum of a distressed Tesla engine made hearing next to impossible. The sound came from behind the doors marked 'Warning! No ferrous metal beyond this point!' Despite the sound, Abigail saw the Captain talking to a short Hindi looking woman in the rubber apron and gloves of an electric worker. With the arm waving and gestures the woman made, it was clear that there was some contention between the two. As they approached, Abigail could hear the woman shouting over the engines.

"And I tell you that we cannot afford to keep all four running! The spikes are getting too great to compensate! Would you rather see Hong Kong in half a month, or an engine room full of melted slag? You cannot have both!" the woman must have seen them approach out of the corner of her eye for she whipped around, confronting Saira. "Who is this? Get away with you! Now, or I'll have you shot! I'll have you both shot!"

"Abigail, Lady Hadley, ROS, Electric Energetics!" Abigail shouted. "How great is your current differential?" she screamed loudly to be heard over the racket.

"I do not care if you are the Queen Mother!" The woman shouted back, "You will," she paused, leaning closer to Abigail. "Did you say, Abigail Hadley? Not the same one who wrote 'Polychrome Transducers as a Step Method' in Oxford Engineering?'

"Yes, that was me!" Abigail shouted back. The older woman straightened up.

"That was not half bad for a theory banger!" She shouted in approval. "Our differential is swinging between 40 and 250 right now. It's been increasing by 20 each swing! The bearings on number four are slipping too much!"

"Wait!" Will shouted, looking between them. "You know her Devi?" Devi turned on him.

"If she is who she says she is, yes!" Devi shouted. "This is the woman you picked up from the fight? Why did you not tell me?" Will waved his hands at her.

"There hasn't been time!" he shouted back. Abigail shouted over them both, grabbing Devi's attention.

"Do you have a variable light clock?" She shouted. Devi waved her hands in negation.

"No!" She shouted back, "Does this look like a toff laboratory? No! And why should we need one? It is the bearings I tell you! We slow the engine down and take it offline!"

"No!" Abigail shouted over the noise, "It could be resonance skip instead! You can't slow her without risking a catastrophic cascade!" Devi looked suddenly very grim.

"Resonance skip?" She shouted back. "Impossible!"

"Damn!" Abigail said. "I had a clock with me on the ship! It's probably burned up and on the ocean floor by now!"

"Hold on here!" Will shouted. "Everybody," he pointed, "hallway, now!" They all trooped out, and when the door closed, the noise mercifully dampened.

"Now," Will spoke into the relative quiet. "Even I know that this skip resonance thing can be real bad. Is there any chance that Hadley here is right, Devi?" The Brahman looked uncomfortably at Abigail.

"Well, it is possible," the Engineer admitted, finally. "Unlikely, but possible."

"Possible?" Will raised an eyebrow, "We need better than that, Devi." The engineer scowled at him and raised her hands in negation. He turned towards Abigail, "And you say that you have a gizmo that could fix this?"

"No," Abigail said exasperatedly. "I had an instrument that could determine how to fix it. Unfortunately, it was on the ship in my instrument trunk!"

Will held up a hand, cutting off her next comment. He turned to Saira and whispered in her ear. Saira looked at him, then the others, and ran off down the corridor.

Will turned back to the two of them. "Lady Abigail Hadley," he continued, "May I present my Chief Engineer,

Devi Neelam, the best one damn engineer on three continents. Devi, you appear to already know our guest."

Abigail nodded her head at Devi, "Chief Engineer Neelam. I apologize for my unseemly entrance. I would not have presumed had I not thought it of serious import." Devi appeared somewhat mollified by this.

"I understand, Lady Hadley," Devi said. "Sure it is that if you are right, then all is proper. It is true that we have not had time to do a thorough resonance calibration in some time. But how can we determine which of us is right in this? We must surely act quickly. This is not a scholarly debate we can be having."

"I know," Abigail frowned in thought. Hesitantly, she ventured, "There is another way to measure the resonant harmony of the four engines, but it will mean removing the outer casings, which has its own dangers." Devi's face held amazement upon hearing this.

"Yes, I would think so!" She exclaimed. "You cannot be thinking what I think you are thinking."

"I can do it myself with some help with the casings," Abigail replied. "As you say, there isn't a lot of time here."

Saira came running back up the corridor, followed by a large man laboring with a trunk.

"That is my equipment trunk!' Abigail exclaimed, as the man set it down between them. She turned on Will, "you didn't tell me you'd rescued it as well," she said accusingly.

"I'm not in the habit of letting unknown castaways have equipment that I can't understand loose on Dancer," the

Captain explained. "I was going to have Devi check it out first."

Abigail flung herself onto her knees, and worked the lock. She quickly rifled through the trunk and pulled up an intricate device in both hands. "Light clock," she held it up for Devi's inspection, who nodded approvingly. Getting to her feet, Abigail said to her, "Do you have a spare set of insulating gloves? "

"Of course," Devi replied. "I have only heard of this technique though. Can you do it on ship-sized Teslas?" Abigail gave a very unladylike snort.

"I have used this on two thousand rated boxes," she replied. "I will need help with your viewing ports though, and we will need to check each one."

"Of course," the older woman nodded in understanding. "Let us get to it then," Devi turned to reenter the engine room. Her head turned to look over her shoulder at the British Scholar.

"You are not proposing to enter my engine room like that, I hope," she observed.

"Of course not, Chief Neelam!" Abigail exclaimed. She began quickly removing her hair pins, her long, red hair came down in tumble. She handed them to Saira, who looked at her in surprise.

"I cannot risk ferrous metal in the engine room. Abigail explained, "You know, pins, eyelets, and such". She dropped her bustle and bent to unlace her boots, which she kicked off. She stood again, unbuttoning her dress. "Help me please," she said quickly to Saira. Saira grabbed her overdress and helped pull it up over her head, then quickly undid her corset. Abigail, standing now in only her chemise and stockings started for the engine room.

"Wait," Will said. He stood un-moving in the hallway with his arms crossed. Devi turned back to him.

"There is no time for suspicions now Captain," Devi said. "Be assured that I will be watching that she does not blow us all up," the engineer finished exasperatedly. Will flung up his hands in surrender towards his chief engineer.

"Alright," he allowed, "but Saira goes in there too to watch her also." The lights dimmed again, and they all looked up.

"Fine," Devi snapped quickly. She addressed Saira, "You stand where I tell you, and do nothing unless I tell you." She looked over Saira's rubber suit and knives with disdain. "Get shed of any metal. That includes those bloody big pig-stickers of yours, and you do not wear that bloody suit in my clean engine room!" Saira nodded and without saying a word, dropped her weapons belt. Devi turned back to Will. "You would help best by reducing us to idle speed, and keeping our altitude level."

"Got it," Will turned and started at a run towards the bridge. Abigail turned to the engineer.

"While I appreciate that we need to remain level, reducing the energy through-put will not have a major effect what we are about to do," she said, puzzled.

"I know," Devi replied. "But otherwise, he will be down here and in our way. It is best to always give a captain something to do, and elsewhere if at all possible. They need to feel useful, you see."

"Oh," Abigail replied in a small voice. Devi opened the door, and the calliope of noise flooding the corridor.

"Now, young Scholar," the Engineer shouted over the din," let us do it!"

~~~

## Upper corridors, Wind Dancer

### Indian Ocean

Some hours later, Saira guided a weary Abigail up to the deck where their cabins were. Saira had been fascinated watching Devi and Lady Hadley work. To be sure, she thought approvingly, the English woman was no stickler for graces. She had gotten her hands dirty with the rest of them, and more than once had stepped under an arch of lightning spitting between two of the tall engines, with no regard for her own safety.

She would make an adjustment that stopped the arch or made it flow differently. It was like watching a story of ancient magicians chaining the sky demons, and made as much sense as well. Finally, the horrible noise had calmed to a dim hum, and as they conferred over gauges and dials, the two women had expressed satisfaction they had gotten the problem 'temporarily resolved'. Devi had told Saira to take Abigail, who was swaying with exhaustion, to bunk out for a watch at least. Despite her protests, she'd allowed Saira to lead her out of the engine room.

"Here we are," Saira said, opening a door. Abigail stood in a small room barely wider than the bed, and looked around dully.

"Like we said," Saira went on, "It is not much. The bed will do, and there's a pot under it. Light switch there, and emergency light there." Saira pointed to places on the walls.

"It is fine," Abigail mumbled. She turned to Saira. "You will wake me, won't you? Those copper inducers really need replacing. No one has used those for years! Your engineer is a miracle worker you know." She yawned, "Oh, pardon me."

"Yes Lady Hadley," Saira grinned at her. "I promise to wake you. You are right, Devi knows her business, but then I am seeing that you do too."

"Call me Abigail," the other woman said with a hand wave, and another yawn.

"Alright Abigail," Saira replied easily. "But now you should lay down for a bit, aiya? Devi will have words, if you show up too tired to stand."

"Yes, I suppose so, at that," Abigail smiled wanly. "She is quite formidable."

"That is one way of expressing it," Saira rolled her eyes. "Do you need anything?"

"No, I will just sit for a minute if you don't mind." Matching action to words, Lady Hadley settled on the edge of the bed.

"All right then," Saira replied. "I am right next door if you need anything." She paused, "Do not try and make your way back there without me, hear?" Abigail waved the comment off.

"I would not dream of trying," she assured the Arms-Master.

"Well, rest well then." Saira closed the door.

Abigail looked around the bare walls, and considered removing her now even filthier chemise. She tested the pallet and found it comfortable. At least it was more comfortable than the storage room had been. Perhaps she would just lie back for a moment first.

There was a noise. Abigail groggily tried to recognize what it was. Was it that Mrs. McDougall, the housekeeper, beating the rugs? No, it was far too loud for that. What then? Suddenly, she remembered everything, the letter from her father, the betrayal, the rescue. She came awake just as the door opened. She opened her eyes to find Saira standing over her.

"Oi," Saira said smiling down at her, "You are a hard one to wake! Do not tell me you slept in your chemise?"

Abigail slowly sat up. Yes, it appeared that she had done just that. Fuzzily, she looked up at the smiling Hindu woman.

"Must you be so bloody cheerful?" Abigail growled. "What time is it?"

"It's just now three bells into day watch," Saira replied. "You have slept much around the clock. Here," she held out a steaming mug of tea. Abigail grabbed it and inhaled the steam rising from it.

"Ah, you may indeed be my savior after all," she sipped the hot tea. It was full of spices that she could not name, sweet and very strong. Saira laughed again.

"Well, if you would sell your soul so cheaply," she replied gaily, "who am I to refuse?"

"You say that I've slept an entire day?" Abigail started to try to stand, tea mug in one hand. The Teslas need those new inserts! You were supposed to wake me!" She felt woozy and sat back down again hard. Saira held out her hands, to help her steady herself, nearly spilling the tea in the process.

"Hold on!" Saira said to her, "Devi said to let you sleep, and to tell you that the 'inserts', whatever those are, will be waiting for you when you get to the engine room. Cap'n Will says 'much obliged for your help', and that you are to clean up and have breakfast, on his orders. Then, if you would be so kind, he requests that you help Devi. I have found you some other clothes to wear, and will take you to the baths, then food, as soon as you have finished your tea."

"Oh, "Abigail replied, feeling somewhat foolish. Saira sat on the edge of the bed silently while she drank. Finishing the tea, she felt less grouchy, and looked up at Saira.

"Thank you," she said, "I can be somewhat difficult when I first wake. My apologies."

"None needed, I assure you!" Saira said reassuringly. "My uncle, now there was a man difficult to wake," she remarked. "His first response was to throw sharp knives at you for waking him!"

"What did you do?" Abigail said.

"Learned to duck," Saira's face broke into a big smile. Abigail found this incredibly amusing for some reason and started laughing. She laughed so hard that tears started down her face as she rocked, before she got herself back under control.

"Oh, my, "she gasped, looking embarrassed. "I can't remember when I last laughed so hard. I am not sure what came over me."

"The wise ones say that laughter is one of the sovereign remedies for the soul," Saira replied still smiling. 'I am glad to see you so."

"Thank you for that," Abigail said wiping her eyes. "You mentioned something about a bath and food?" She looked down at her chemise. "I suppose that I should dress. It would not do to wonder about the ship half-naked." Saira looked at her in puzzlement.

"I do not see that you are even half-naked." She observed. "And I should remind you that you have already wandered the ship, dressed as you are. I have brought an assortment of clothing for you if you wish it." She held up a pair of pants.

"Oh, but I couldn't wear that," Lady Hadley protested, "it shows off my legs!" Saira cocked her head to one side to stare at her.

"And how would it not?" she asked. 'I wear them. Would you rather climb a ladder with the next person looking up your backside?"

"Oh well," Abigail replied flustered. "That was necessary before, and you look very proper and...and martial." She gulped her tea, refusing to meet Saira's eye.

"No one was really looking on the ladders were they?" Abigail asked somewhat plaintively. Saira regarded her solemnly.

"I did not pay attention," the Arms-Master said dryly. "I am certain that no one had a shocking revelation upon seeing something new if they did so." Abigail grimaced at this and drained her tea mug.

"Right you are," she said stoutly. "Well, I can do this if you can stand to be seen with me." Saira smiled at her.

"That is the spirit!" Saira exclaimed. She picked up the other clothes. "I shall bring these along to change into after the bath then." Abigail nodded at her, if not enthusiastically than at least determinedly. She stood up.

"Lead on then!" she said.

Making their way down the corridors, Abigail was pleasantly surprised to find that they did not meet anyone as she walked in her underwear. They did not, thankfully, climb any ladders, and soon found themselves in front of a pair of large redwood and brass doors.

Abigail stopped, her heart suddenly pounding. She remembered what Saira had said before. "Communal baths?" she said involuntarily. She realized that she had been running around the ship in just her chemise and stockings, but this seemed different somehow.

"Yes, as I mentioned before I believe," Saira replied deadpan. "After you," she gave a little bow towards the door.

Well, Abigail thought, do as the natives do. She took a deep breath and opened the door.

The room was the first one lit only by oil light that she'd seen on the ship. There were two large round tubs each big enough to hold five or six people she figured. One had steam rising from it. Around the wall were narrow benches and pegs she assumed where for hanging clothes on. And the room was completely empty. She turned to find Saira looking at her with a straight face.

"I perhaps forgot to mention that there is almost nobody ever here after second bell of day watch," she said. "I thought that you might wish to be private given your English ways. I can leave you also if you wish. "Abigail balled her hands into fists and exhaled slowly.

"Saira," Abigail ground out, "do people often express a wish to strangle you?" The young woman's teeth gleamed back at her in the lamp light.

"More often than you might think," Saira said easily. "Why I cannot imagine." The dark-skinned woman looked at her sideways with an impish smile. "I could wash your back for you instead if you wish." Abigail startled at that. Her view of herself as being very modern and liberated was getting a rather severe testing, she thought ruefully as she cast about for what to say.

"No, I . . . thank you," she stammered, trying to think of what would be polite in the situation. Finally, she decided that she really did not want to be alone. She looked at the Arms-Master uncertainly. "Ah, I would not mind someone to talk with though, if you would care to join me." Saira nodded. Although it was probably just the bonding effect of bespelling the woman into rapport, she found herself feeling for the Englishwoman. She sat down on a bench and began undoing her boots.

"No worries," Saira said. "I am familiar with your mudfoot English ways, and I am very good with the talking. Besides, you are in a strange place with strange people, and not sure what is what, yes? The offer stands though; I also do very good back washing."

Feigning a nonchalance that she didn't really feel, Abigail undressed, washed off with a sponge and a bucket of water over a grate, and stepped her way into the steaming pool. She hissed at the heat of the water, but it soon relaxed muscles that she hadn't realized were sore. Saira finished undressing. Abigail was startled to see that she had tattoos. One was on her arm, an image of a winged globe, and one of an opening flower sat on her mons veneris, which was denuded of hair. Abigail had seen pictures of Indian temple statues, so it was not really shocking, although she had always thought those were poetic license. Saira meanwhile ignored Abigail's momentary stare, and chatted away amiably, climbing in across from her. Soon the two were talking away as if they were old friends.

Abagail learned many things as they talked. She learned that 'Cap'n Will' had taken Saira on when she had been destitute, or 'beached' as she called it, nearly two years earlier in Seattle Freeport. That Captain Hunting Owl was not wealthy by any means, but along with Lawrence Rogers, had obtained the Wind Dancer about five years ago, in a manner that was still mysterious. She learned that according to Saira, the crew thought the world of the Captain.

She learned that the ship usually had between fifty and sixty crew, including officers. They were slightly under that at the moment, which was how the cabin next to Saira's was vacant. She learned that Mr. Rogers, the ships' First Officer was considered a bit humorless and stiff, but fair in his job. She learned that life as an 'airdevil' on a fighting ship was at times boring, exciting, bawdy, and uncertain. She learned that Saira had many lovers, both on the ship and off the ship. Saira spoke of her exploits in such an openly shameless manner that Abigail wasn't sure if she was appalled or envious of her.

Saira was also a very good listener, for all her brash manner. Abigail found herself talking about the difficulties of being a woman at New Oxford, her triumph at becoming a Royal Scholar, her own liaisons, and her struggles against social expectations. She spoke of her father and the dream he had that had become her own, a dream of finding new ways of power generation. One that would bring civilization to everyone on the planet. She stopped herself when she realized that she was about to talk about her current mission to China, and sat upright in the water.

"Goodness," she said smiling, "I do apologize for running on. Perhaps the Captain was right and you are a sorceress who is bespelling me." She meant it to be humorous, but was surprised when Saira replied seriously.

"I am what you would call a sorceress," Saira said solemnly. "I promise though that I am not using the power on you now, nor will I unless you seek harm to me or mine." Abigail shook her head in disbelief at this.

"I can never tell when you are joking," Abigail said lightly.

"I am not joking," Saira replied. "I am what you would call a priestess of the Naga, the Serpent People, as was my mother, and her mother before her." She shrugged "I am not a very good one, as I refused to follow my mother's wish for power." She pointed to her lower tattoo, "This says that I am dedicated to the path. Sometimes I can see the flow of the world river, what you call the future. I can sometimes change it. I see into the hearts of others at times, and honor the Gods in the ways I was trained to do. Mostly I follow the red path, which means that I am very good at fighting and frigging." She said this last with a rakish grin. Abigail was stunned by this revelation. She had seen the other woman as someone very practical, and down to earth if rebellious against convention, not given to, well, superstitions for lack of a better word.

"I'm afraid that I do not believe in magic," Abigail said slowly, not wishing to offend her new friend. Saira laughed at this pronouncement.

"No worries Abigail," she replied merrily. "I know lots of people who do not believe in your science either. I think we will do fine." The tone of four chimes cut through the air. "Oy," Saira said, "that is fourth bell. Time we got a move on! Are you hungry?"

Abigail found that she was, and pushing aside the disturbing thoughts she had, climbed out of the water. The choices of clothing that Saira had brought were, to be charitable, interesting. A couple of 'dresses' were of such scandalous cut that she would never think of wearing them outside a bedroom. Others were hardly practical, given that she would be climbing ladders and had no other foundation garments, as

Saira had pointed out. She reluctantly settled on something similar to what she had seen the other women of the crew wearing, pants of a durable cotton weave, a tunic-like shirt, and a vest. She had only her heeled ankle boots for shoes, unlike the other's rubber soled high boots. Saira allowed as they would work as long as she was careful. Saira finally handed her a pair of goggles to place around her neck and a cylinder to place in a pouch in her vest.

"Should we get breached, Gods forbid," she explained, "the air can go out very fast and it can be very cold. Put the goggles over your eyes, and the cylinder to your mouth, like so." She demonstrated. "You will have about five minutes, which should be long enough to get to safety. I will show you how to charge it from a reserve tank later."

"How will I know where safety is?" Abigail asked.

Saira looked at her mournfully, "If it is not obvious, then you are likely buggered anyway."

"Oh, I see." Abigail reflected that flying was perhaps not as safe as she had been lead to believe as a coddled passenger on a liner. At least, she thought to herself with satisfaction, Saira was not coddling her.

The main mess was emptier than Abigail would have thought, until Saira explained that they were "two bells" off watch change and that most had eaten already and either gone on station or elsewhere. The smell of cooking food reminded Abigail's stomach that she was desperately hungry, and hoped that there would be something to eat. Saira walked up to the open window at one end and rapped on the sill.

"Wu," she cried out. An Oriental man with the lined face of age came to the window.

"You too late," he said with a dismissive wave of his hands. "Only porridge and tea left. You sleep too long!"

"Now Wu my love," Saira pouted, "after all we have been working hard to save the ship!" He grunted at her unimpressed. "Let me introduce you by the way," Saira turned so that Wu could see Abigail. "This is the famous Lady Abigail Hadley who worked all night to keep your old hide from being blown all over the South China Sea. Lady Abigail," she continued formally, "this is the ship's doctor and head cook, Dr. Wu Ling Ma."

"Dr. Wu," Abigail bowed her head and spoke the only Mandarin she knew which was a formal greeting, or so she'd been told. The old man's face lit up with a smile. He said another phrase that Abigail didn't know and bowed back.

"I'm sorry," Abigail replied somewhat flustered, "that was the only Mandarin I know." His smile widened as he waved a hand in dismissal.

"That alright," he replied in English. "Your accent good. I will teach you more, if you wish. Now, what fruit would you like on porridge?"

"Fruit?" Abigail pondered for a moment and then asked uncertainly, "Do you have mango by chance?"

He smiled again and vanished. They heard the sound of rapid chopping. He reappeared with two bowls with steam rising from them. Abigail took hers and saw that he had arranged thin slices of mango fruit in a wheeled pattern on top of the steaming porridge, which smelled wonderful.

"It's beautiful!" She said to him, "Thank you." He nodded still smiling at her. Saira took her bowl, and then looked at Wu.

"Why do I not have the bounty of your art as well, oh great artist?" Saira asked.

"Your job to keep ship safe" Wu mock scowled at Saira. "Lady Abigail is guest, and must be shown honor. Besides," he shrugged, "it was the last of the mango. You live."

"Old quack!" Saira laughed.

"Hussy arm-breaker!" he smiled back, then tossed her an apple which she plucked out of the air. Saira took a big bite out of it.

"Much obliged," she said around the mouthful. He waved and turned away from the window. Saira pointed with her apple at a free space at the long table in front of them.

"Let us sit here and I will get us tea," she suggested. Abigail placed her bowl down on the table across from Saira.

"Allow me," Abigail volunteered, and moved back to the large urns by the window. She filled two mugs from the spigots, looked in vain for any white to add to them, and returned with two spoons as well.

"Ah, thank you," Saira beamed. "I was just going to mention that we needed spoons as well." She took first a mug and then one of the offered utensils. She smiled, shaking her head.

"What is it?" Abigail asked as she sat across from her.

"Oh, I was just thinking of the last time I was waited on by British nobility." She cocked her head to one side as if thinking. "That would be . . . never!" She smiled at Abigail.

"I do wish you would not carry on so about that. After all..." she searched for the right phrase, "I put my bloomers on one leg at a time just as you do."

"But you know now that I do not wear bloomers," Saira said innocently. Abigail waved her spoon at her.

"Oh stop that! You know what I mean!" Abigail spooned up some of the porridge. It tasted amazing. There were some sort of sweet spices and chopped nuts in it that set off the mango wonderfully. "Oh my," she exclaimed, "this is really quite good." Saira grinned around her own spoon.

"Wu does good by us when he can. Speaking of which, you made an admirer I noticed." She wiggled her eyebrows.

"Is he really also the ship's doctor as well as cook?" Abigail asked before spooning up more. She'd figured out that Saira's comments were largely good natured poking at her, probably a sign of camaraderie. Abigail just wasn't always sure how to respond yet.

"Aiya," Saira replied taking another bite of apple, "and very good at both. It makes sense if you think of it. He has studied his whole life what makes the body well. That should include what keeps it well, yes?"

"I hadn't thought of that, "Abigail said. "There's wisdom in that I can see. If he really does heal as well as he cooks, I can imagine he must be very good indeed." Saira nodded.

"It is no exaggeration to say he has saved my life on more than one occasion," the woman vowed. She set her apple core into her empty bowl, and reached for her mug. Abigail looked down in surprise to see that she had eaten all of her own bowl as well. Saira leaned towards Abigail across the table.

"I have had a vision," she began seriously, "and wish to ask you a question." Abbigail sipped from her mug, containing her natural skepticism.

"A vision of the future?" Abigail asked. "Do you have them often?"

"I am having more of them of late," Saira said with a shrug. "It happens when there is going to be a large change in the flow of life."

"I would think that there is always change in the...how did you put it? Yes, 'the flow of life'" she sipped again. "Do they always come true?" Saira shrugged again.

"Sometimes yes," she said. "Sometimes I do not always understand what I see, or I am mistaken." She smiled at Abigail. "You say it well for all that you do not believe it yourself. There is always change in the flow, and I would not be prideful enough to mistake that I can see all. None that is human truly can. But sometimes I am gifted with a small seeing. To understand this one well, I must ask you a question."

"Well," Abigail said putting down her mug. She braced for some strange sort of fortune teller claptrap. "What do you wish to ask?"

A shadow came between them at the table. Abigail looked up to see a brown-skinned woman with many braids standing at the table end. She was dressed much as they were in pants and a tunic with vest, a pair of goggles perched on top of her unruly braids.

"Arms-Master," the woman said, to Saira, very deliberately not looking at Abigail. "I understand that you wish me to undertake the Tigers' morning trainings." Saira nodded.

"That is correct Tikku," she smiled up at the younger woman. "I think that you are ready for this. It will only be for a few days while I tend to our guest here," she nodded towards Abigail. "Let me introduce you." She held her palm up towards Abigail, "This is the Lady Abigail Hadley a member of the British Royal Order of Scholars." She held up her other palm towards Tikku.

"Lady Hadley," she said. "You may remember Tikku from the boarding of Hu Fan's ship. This is Tikku Talaton, one of the best fighters in my Tigers." Tikku bobbed her head towards Abigail.

"Thank you for your action in my rescue, Tikku," Abigail said with a smile.

"Lady Hadley," Tikku said shortly. She then looked at Saira again silently. As the silence stretched out, Abigail opened her mouth simply in an attempt to fill the silence. Saira abruptly picked up her mug and addressed the standing woman with narrowed eyes.

"Simply have them all practice leap-frogging under cover after first exercises," She said crisply. "I was not satisfied with how they did on our last boarding. We could be faster. Is there anything else?" The braids shook in negation.

"No Arms-Master," Tikku replied. She bobbed her head coolly towards Abigail. "A pleasure to see you again Lady

Hadley." Abigail leaned towards Saira as the other woman walked out the mess doors.

"I am sorry," she said to the Arms-Master. "Is there something that I should have done? I do not intent any insult." Saira's gaze had followed Tikku as she left the mess. She turned towards the Scholar.

"Do not let her attitude bother you," the Hindi woman said to her. "I believe that it is simply because you are British that she had difficulty with the British." Abigail frowned at this.

"I see," she said slowly, looking at the Arms-Master directly. "Is there likely to be much difficulty with this?" Saira opened her mouth to speak, and then frowned as she looked over Abigail's shoulder.

"Ah," she exhaled softly. "And now here would come our Mr. Rogers to pay his respects, I imagine." She reached out and touched Abigail's hand. "Please, we will speak more of this later if that is alright with you." Touched, Abigail took her hand and squeezed it.

"Of course, Saira," she assured her. Abigail was about to say more when a polite cough forced her to turn. She saw a tall thin man dressed all in black with graying blonde hair that came to his shoulders. His face seemed to be set in a permanent frown.

"Arms-Master," the man said to Saira with short nod. He faced Abigail and gave her a short but more formal bow. "Lady Hadley, I am First Officer Rogers. If I would not be interrupting, I would like a moment of your time."

"Of course, Mr. Rogers," Abigail said cordially. "Please," she indicated with her hand, "do be seated, sir." Saira scooped up both their bowls quickly.

"I will turn these in then." She said briefly. Looking at her, Saira asked Abigail, "more tea?"

"No thank you," Abigail smiled at her. "Would you care for tea, Mr. Rogers?" Rogers looked startled at this.

"No thank you," he said with a glance that went between Saira and herself. "I am on duty, and would only stay for a moment." Saira wordlessly picked up the bowls and glided off.

Abigail had caught the by-play or rather lack of it, wondering it what was it with the crew of this ship that they were so emotional.

"Is there some problem, Mr. Rogers?" She asked him.

"No, not at all," he said in a tone that indicated that there was. "I simply wanted to see how you were getting on, Milady. I understand that you have been working in the engine rooms. I must tell you that that isn't really required of you. I promise. Certainly not after all you've been through."

Oh dear, Abigail thought. The last thing she expected to find on a ship of bloodthirsty killers was an officer concerned for her station. She fervently prayed that wasn't the case here. She smiled.

"I assure you Mr. Rogers that it was quite at my insistence," she emphasized the word, "that I have been aiding in your engine room. As you may know I am a Scholar in Energetics, and find the opportunity to practice very rewarding. Your engineer, Devi Neelam, runs a wonderful operation. I've been very grateful for her indulgence." Rogers harrumphed at that and then glanced quickly at her clothes. It was only a glance, but Abigail could see what was on his mind.

"I'm sure Milady that we can find you something more suitable to wear if you wish." He smiled at her as if in pain. Oh my, Abigail thought, in despair, he really was so Old School. Perhaps it would be best to confront him directly.

"Mr. Rogers," she said gently, "are you concerned for my modesty?" He harrumphed again, not looking at her.

"Well, Milady, these are hardly conditions that you're used to I'm sure," he said earnestly, then looked her in the eye. "I wouldn't want you to get the idea that we're all like Arms-Master Brighton, or that tolerating such behavior is required of someone of your station, I promise you it isn't."

"I see," Abigail replied, now feeling rather nettled by his attitude. While it was all very well to have concern for her feelings, she had dealt before with other's expectations of how she should conduct herself according to her station. That he impugned her new friend the Arms-Master did not incline her to be tolerant of him. She straightened up and stared at him across the table.

"I notice that you have several women aboard this ship Mr. Rogers," she said coolly. "I notice none of them in skirts fanning themselves, but rather carrying out their duties in practical garments such as what I am wearing. I am hardly the fanning sort myself. My honor demands that I give aid to my rescuers both as I am able, and as I choose. As for Saira, Arms-Master Brighton that is, I can assure you that I find her both eminently satisfactory as a companion, and as an example of your crew." Rogers smiled thinly at that.

"Frankly Milady," he said dryly, "Saira Brighton is an undisciplined harlot and a heathen." He continued, undeterred as Abigail visibly bristled at his statement. "She's also one of the best fighters that I've ever seen, a natural leader, and a true asset to this ship, not including her hocus pocus." His shoulders twitched slightly, "Which I will leave you to decide the merits of." He leaned forward with a thin smile, "And if you tell her I said that I will deny it loudly." Abigail shook her head in wonder at this pronouncement, and opened her mouth to speak, only to have Rogers hold up a hand which prevented her from doing so.

"I meant no disrespect to you, Milady," he said dryly. "I only wished to assure myself that you felt that you are being well treated and are comfortable." He smiled thinly again. "I believe that you have put my concerns to rest." He stood up, and bowed to her again. "Should you have any concerns or needs, you have only to ask, Milady. Now if you will excuse me, I must return to my duties." Abigail watched as he walked out of the mess. Saira came over to her and raised an eyebrow in silent question.

"That is a very unique man," Abigail said in reply. Saira grinned at her.

"That he is," she agreed. "The Captain is perhaps the soul of the ship, Devi the heart." She flexed a muscle. "I may be perhaps the hands, but that man is the sinew which makes the ship run." Saira leaned close to her, "and if you ever tell the British prig with the stick up his arse I said this, I shall deny it," Saira said seriously. Abigail laughed at this, and shook her head again at Saira's look.

"You are all rather . . . unique I think." Abigail stood up, "Still I'm glad to have met you all. Thank you for a wonderful breakfast." Saira stood with her and inclined her head.

"You are most welcome. I have a feeling that we will all be saying the same," Saira returned. "Now, can you find your way to the engine room on your own? I have things that I need to do that do not require that I stand around the engine room naked all day. Not of course, that I am not inspiring doing so." She mimed primping her short dark hair.

"Not to mention modest!" Abigail smiled. "I am sure that I can find my way. But what will your Captain Will say if I am without my guardian?"

"I have never found much use for what you English call modesty," Saira allowed. "Both Cap'n Will and I think that you are ready to be on your own. We have talked about this. You do not put on airs, the crew knows who you are by now, and Devi says that you're a miracle worker that the engines need." She cocked her head to one side to regard the British Scholar. "Besides, we figure that if you were going to blow up the ship, or try to assassinate one of us, you would have given yourself away by now."

Abigail blinked at this rather stark answer. She had been at first busy trying to determine if they meant her harm, then so absorbed by the problem of the engines, that she hadn't considered that they might have concerns about her.

"I see," Abigail said slowly. "Thank you for your trust."

"No worries," Saira said turning to go. She whipped her head back just before the mess doors. "Just do not prove us wrong," she smiled and was gone. Abigail wasn't sure how to interpret the smile that accompanied those words.

# Chapter Nine

## Main Mess Hall, *Wind Dancer*

Tikku walked into the mess, weary from a long day. First she had to direct the Tiger exercises, because the Arms-Master was babysitting some British toff they had picked up from the battle, then she spent the rest of her day looking to rigging duties under Chief Bobby. The Chief Rigger had made no bones about him wanting every inch of Wind Dancer inspected for battle damage. Which meant that Tikku had squatted for hours inspecting the hull while secured by only the safety ropes. It was hard, dangerous work which left you tired down to your bones.

She was startled to see the English 'Scholar' sitting alone at one end of a long mess table. She was wearing airdevil togs clearly in an attempt to ape her betters, Tikku thought. Well it wasn't going to work with her, she vowed. Coming from Jakarta as she did, she knew all about British trickery and snobbery. Her people had been taken twice over, first by the Dutch and then by the English. The English were a tricky lot, and none more so than the upper classes like Lady Whats-her-name.

Tikku stalked over to the tea station and grabbed a hot mug. She saw a group she knew sitting at the other end of Miss Fancypants' table and called out a greeting to them, then walked back as they cleared a spot for her on the long bench that served as mess hall seating.

"Here now Tikku," Greeted Roger a fellow rigger, hosting his tea mug. "Friggin' hard day checking out for battle damage eh?" Tikku shrugged at this. She gave a sidelong glance at the British woman as she sat down.

"I do not know about that Rog," she replied loudly. "At least it's honest work. Not like some folks who just loll around, living off the sweat of others." She sipped her tea, turning back towards Roger. Roger's current bedmate, a young man who worked up in engineering, leaned towards her with a hiss.

"Lay off, Tikku," he said in a low voice. "I heard from Chief Neelam herself that Lady Hadley worked all yesterday to keep the ship from having a cascade failure. She's earned her berth." Tikku looked down her nose at him.

"Likely an English trick," she announced in the same loud voice. "It's common knowledge that they trick anyone who's not them when you're not looking. Aye, and steals from them too!" This last pronouncement was met by an uncomfortable silence among her mates. Tikku slammed her mug on the table.

"What?" She demanded of her fellow airdevils, "You know what I say is true!" A voice came from the far end of the table.

"Would that also apply to your own First Officer as well?" Abagail inquired mildly. Tikku jumped up, stalking down the tables' length towards her.

"You leave the FO out of this," she yelled stabbing with her finger. "You are just trying to trick me into violatin' the Articles!" She raised both her arms in appeal to the room.

"Can no one see how dangerous it is letting a toff around run loose on the ship?" she asked them. Abagail looked up at her coolly, her mug still half way to her lips.

"There is a scientific answer to your question you know," she said calmly to the angry airdevil. Tikku lowered her arms, and sneered at her, while placing her hands on her hips.

"Oh?" she said, "And what would that be?" The Scholar carefully lowered her mug to the table.

"Get stuffed," Lady Hadley said in a loud clear voice. The silence in the mess hall that followed this calm obscenity was absolute. Tikku simply stared at her, her mouth hanging open. Then Roger whooped at this, laughing and pounding the table in front of him.

"She had you there, Tikku!" He announced gleefully. "Too bad you don't like the fillies so you can't take her up on it!" This earned him a general round of laughter which caused the Indonesian woman to freeze in place.

"I will see to you," Tikku said to Abigail with a hiss. She turned about and stalked from the mess, laughter following her. Roger stood up and offered Abigail Tikku's spot on the bench. After a moment's hesitation, she rose to accept. Roger smiled at her as she settled down.

"That was more than a bit alright," he said to her. The others sitting at the table agreed with murmurs and nods.

"Thank you," Abigail said. "I fear however that I have made something of an enemy over it." Roger shook his head.

"You have to give Tikku no mind. By the time you see her again she'll have passed it off," he said to her. "She's always setting up to fight with someone. Best thing that ever happened to her was getting into the Tigers. She's full of fight she is." Again the murmurs and nods of agreement from the others seated around the end of the table. "Besides, we aint at all prejudiced," he reassured her. "We don't care if you was born of the silk crowd. You seem more than a bit alright to us for the fixin' of the engines. Roger Bates is the name, Rigger Second Class, welcome aboard." He lifted his mug towards her. "Cheers." Abigail raised hers in kind.

"Cheers," she replied with a smile.

# Chapter Ten

Upper Corridor, *Wind Dancer*

South China Sea

The following days were some of the happiest that Abigail had ever known. Devi Neelam turned out to have a wealth of practical knowledge about Tesla engines that Abigail had never encountered before, neither in books nor from lectures at college. Every day brought a new challenge and new learning. She was also pleased to find that there was much that she knew that Devi did not, and together they added several improvements that Abigail was quite proud of. Not the kind of things that one could write up for a journal perhaps, but solid engineering work.

Saira had pulled her away a couple of times to show her different areas of the ship. She had gained a new appreciation for airships and those who crewed them. She was especially impressed by the 'riggers', the men and women who climbed out on the hull itself to inspect and maintain it. Perhaps it was because she could never imagine doing so herself. She even grew accustomed to enjoying the communal baths, something that had been outside her experience beforehand. Now she wondered why such a thing was not done by everyone.

She did not see much of the Captain during this time. Saira mentioned something about negotiations taking his attention. She was very surprised then to see him waiting for her when she closed the engineering door behind her. He was leaning against the wall, clad in his usual leather pants, linen shirt, and sleeveless vest. He seemed to be always wearing the large pistol at his hip. The many small brass discs embedded in the vest reflected the light as he stood to greet her.

"Captain Hunting Owl," she greeted him. "What brings you down to engineering?"

"Working somewhat late aren't you Lady Abigail? He asked. "How are my engines?" She noticed that one of her braids had come lose and began to re-do them.

"Oh, I assure you they're fine. I was just rewiring some of your conjunction relays. You should now have an additional million watts or so per cycle. I understand that should be helpful to you." She finished re-winding her braids, setting them in place with the bone pins she'd borrowed from Devi.

"Very helpful," Will agreed. "But I thought that Devi would have told you to knock off for the day some time ago."

"Well, she did mention some kind of event, but I really needed to finish the rewiring. I'm not much for parties, you see." She finished somewhat awkwardly.

Will crossed his arms and frowned at her, creases written in his dark face.

"I am concerned for you, Lady Hadley," he announced. He cocked his head to one side, "I've heard that all you've done the last three days is work down here, eat, and sleep. Forgive me but I'm a blunt sort. Are you alright? Anything that I should know about?" Abigail felt the heat rising to her cheeks. Damned complexion, she thought to herself.

"Oh no Captain," she replied, "everyone and everything has been most excellent. You have a very professional engine crew and a beautiful ship." She took a breath and confessed. 'To be perfectly honest, I so seldom get to work on real equipment that does real functions that I find it incredibly satisfying."

He nodded, giving her the boyish grin that Abigail had seen on their first meeting. "Well, Wind Dancer aims to please. Devi certainly has had nothing but good things to say about what you've done for us. I must insist that you accompany me now though. It's not just 'an event' it's Second Day. Consider it a Captain's order."

He held out his arm still smiling, and patiently waited her response. He really was rather charming for a mercenary killer, Abigail thought to herself. Then she realized that she had been bathing and eating with mercenary killers for days now. Coming to a decision, she placed her arm in his, and smiled back.

"Second Day?" she asked him, as they started walking, "I am not familiar with it." She was acutely aware of the smudges on her face, and the fact that she needed another bath after working in the heat of the engine room.

"No need to get all cleaned up or anything," he reassured her as if divining her thoughts. "Most crew will be coming either right off shift, or it's just before they start one, so it isn't fancy. You are fitting in so well that I forgot that you would not know about Second Day. As for what it is," he shrugged. "It simply means that we're about two days out from landing. The party is supposed to bring good luck for the landing.

Story has it that it goes all the way back to Admiral von Zeppelin and the first Victory. When they were two days out from London, they had a sort of a 'hurray, it looks like we'll make it' party." He shrugged again. "Makes sense of a sort. They would be going into battle pretty much at landfall, so why not let the crew blow off some tension two days before they reached their destination? Anyway, most air devils keep it now. Sometimes it's only a drink at mess, sometimes more, especially on longer flights. God help the captain that tries to not let the crew have the party." He grinned at her again, "We're a superstitious lot really. Besides after the battle with Hu Fan they've earned a bit of fun. They're a good crew."

"I see," Abigail said, taking this in. "May I ask why you refer to yourselves as 'air devils'? It seems a strange self-naming to me."

Will laughed, "Again it's an old saying going back to the War. Your Christian Way has these spirits that are called 'angels', and one of them fell from the skies and was called a 'devil' thereafter yes? Became the bad spirit when he did so, right? And some day he is supposed to storm the heavens, no?"

"Well, yes," Abigail blinked. "That's more or less right. There's much more to the story though."

Will nodded wisely, "There always is." He shook his head, "I've had people try to explain the Christ Way to me, and it's even more confusing than the Hindi Ways that Saira talks about. Don't you see though," he said seriously to her, "that's what we do; we 'storm the heavens'. Every day." He stopped talking as they continued walking, and then turned back to her grinning "And we're as likely to fall and be damned when all is said and done. So," he asked, "how are you getting on with the crew?"

Abigail laughed at the question.

"At first I think some where a bit uncertain as to how I would take their rather liberal use of profanity. However, after I called Tikku 'a banging slot' in response to her comments, things seemed to relax considerably." Will missed a step and stared at her.

"You said what?" He sputtered at her.

Abigail just looked at him.

"Please, Captain," she said, "I am a Scholar, not a nun, after all."

Will nodded.

"Right," he said, clearly recovering from his surprise. "Well, that's the way to handle Tikku."

"Oh, she is really a bit alright once you establish what is what," Abigail said. "If I may, it seems to me that you have a most amazing crew. After the War, much was said about all mankind becoming brothers."

Will gave a snort at that statement as they continued walking.

"Precisely, my point," Abigail nodded at his response. "While much is said about brotherhood, it is my perception that action seldom follows from that." She remembered her encounter with colonial prejudice at the Air Tower in

Bombay with a dull anger. "In fact, much the opposite. To our common disgrace I might add. Yet here on Wind Dancer I see men and women of every possible origin working and living together. How do you manage this?"

Will laughed, and pulled thoughtfully on his braid while they walked.

"Well, it's not from any 'noble ideal', I can tell you that," he said thoughtfully. "Lots of airships are similar. We don't have time for foolishness." His brow furled as he gathered his thoughts. "The War changed a lot of things, I am guessing. Men and women were swept up from wherever they were. They fought together, and then died together. In the air, where you came from, what color you were, or what you had between your legs, wasn't as important as if you could stand by your salt, and do your job well."

"After the War, many tried to go back to what they'd been before. Many did in fact." He shrugged, "But some couldn't either." He grinned at her ruefully, "We're the misfits, I guess. Some of the olders found that home wasn't what they remembered, or liked the air life better. Some of the youngers are half-breeds from the War and have no place, or grew up on an airship, sometimes both things, like me." He grinned at her again. Some devils start as mudfoots who don't fit in." He waved to take in all of the ship around them. "Except up here, except in the sky."

Abigail nodded at this, thinking as they ascended the main port stairs. From the direction of the mess hall she heard the sounds of music and laughter. As they came closer, she saw a man and woman stagger arm in arm out of the mess doors, the noise inside cut off like a knife as the doors closed behind them. She heard Will chuckle softly. "Looks as if someone started the celebration early," he murmured to her. As they approached the couple, Abigail saw that both of them appeared to be trying to hold each other up as very drunken mates will tend to do.

"Cap'n!" the woman slurred, drunkenly. She pulled away from the man, waving vaguely behind them. "I think that they're warmed up and ready to lift!"

The man stood, slightly weaving, nearer the wall. He touched his forehead to Will in salute. "Beggin' your pardon for starting early, Cap'n", he said with the exaggerated care that very intoxicated people are prone to. "But with your permission, me and Sandy here have some private matters to  discuss." Will shook his head, regarding them both gravely.

"While private discussions are private," Will agreed, "I would appreciate you both clearing my hallways. Neither of you are in any shape to be walking them. Now git, off with you both." His smile took some of the sting out of his words. The look of relief on the young man's face was comical, while the woman simply smiled at the Captain, taking the young man's arm in her own again.

As they squeezed past Abigail and Will in the narrow corridor, the man murmured a quick 'Lady Hadley'. The woman echoed the greeting as she passed Abigail. Will turned to watch them as they went, then called out, his hands cupped to his mouth.

"Ravin! Sandy!" he said. "This does not mean that you are excused from duty tomorrow! I expect you both at you stations in the morning!" They both raised their hands without turning.

"Aye, Aye, Cap'n!" they chorused, and then staggered off down the hallway together. Will watched them go, shaking his head.

"Youthful spirits," he explained, seeing the look on Abbie's face at this encounter. "The whole party won't be like they are," he reassured her. He held out his arm towards her again. "Well Lady Abigail, shall we go in?"

Abigail swallowed, remembering again the salacious 'penny-dreadfuls' of Mrs. McDougal, her housekeeper, and what they said about air pirate parties. She reminded herself again that nothing untoward had happened to her so far on the cruise. Smiling bravely, she took his arm.

"Of course," she said gamely. Will looked at her as if he wasn't fooled, but led them towards the double doors anyway.

The room beyond was hot and full of smoke. Lively music came from a makeshift dais that had been set up at one end of the room, the other occupants banging on their tables in time to the music.

There were a half dozen people on the dais with different instruments, including Devi Neelam. Devi was sitting with a multi-stringed instrument that made soaring patterns of music that wove in and out of the flutes, pipes and drums of the others. The tables had been pushed against the walls leaving a clear space in front of the stage where two men danced a jig together. She scanned the crowd of people and saw Saira stand up from one table, waving them over.

She exchanged nods and smiles with others she didn't know as they wove their way to towards the table. To her confusion they all appeared to know her though. The captain shouted over the noise while releasing his arm, "Lady Hadley, have a seat!" He gestured to the bench beside him.

As she settled, she returned greetings from the others at the table. Saira was sitting on the lap of a dark skinned man, both of them clad in silk robes of blue and green. Saira gave a small wave of her hand. She saw others at the table who were unknown to her. There was a short ginger haired man with a ruddy complexion who scowled a nod, next to him a blonde woman who waved, and a grizzled old man who touched his forehead. Another man dropped two short dark bottles in front of them.

"Thank you, Captain," she shouted back.

"Call me Will," the captain said. "There's no rank in the mess."

"Will," she nodded, "In that case please call me Abigail." She pointed to the bottle, "What is this?"

"Rum ration," He explained. "You're about three days overdue." He popped the cork on the bottle for her and handed it back. He stood up and raised his own bottle over his head. Gradually the noise of conversation stopped. The musicians ended on a flourish. In the silence, everyone rose to their feet holding a drink. Abigail followed suit. Will's voice rang out over the room.

"Well shipmates, once again we reach a Second Day," he paused for a moment. "This one has been a touch more hairy than some, I will allow." Chuckles ran around the room at this. Will waited for them to die down before continuing, "But you all can take pride in the fact that a scum dog like Hu Fan won't be plyin' his trade anymore." A surf wave of agreement met his words. "Here's to a safe landing and to Queen Victoria!" He tipped his bottle towards his lips.

"Safe landing and Queen Victoria!" The room rang with the chorus. Almost as one, the room upended their drinks.

Abigail took a drink, feeling the dark sweet liquor burn its way down her throat. It was strong enough to bring tears to her eyes, but she held her dignity. Everyone sat again and the musicians took up where they left off.

"Abigail," Will said over the music, "this is some of the bridge crew that you haven't met yet. Let me do introductions." He pointed to the blonde who was wearing a fancy dress in dark blue. "Naomi Walters, our bridge talker. It's her voice that you've heard over the speaker horns."

"Lady Hadley," Naomi nodded towards her over her bottle. Abigail had a good ear for accents; Naomi's speech had the sound of a British finishing school.

"Will was just telling me there's no rank in the mess, so call me Abigail, please." She smiled over the music. The younger woman blushed a deeper red and nodded, smiling shyly back.

"Michael McGuire, Our Aetherwave operator," Will pointed to the ginger haired man.

The man tipped his bottle in an ironic salute. "Abigail," the man said in an Irish brogue you could cut with a knife. Clearly, he had already had more than one of the potent bottles.

"That fearsome looking man under Saira is Jarro, our helmsman". The dark skinned man's face was covered in elaborate tattoos that made a snarling mask. He silently waved a hand.

"Our Arms-Master you already know, of course." Saira lifted a bottle in salute towards Abigail. Will gestured towards the man on his left, "This old scoundrel," Will finished, "is Bobby Marsh, our Chief Rigger." The old man's dark face split into a wide grin as he spoke to her over the noise.

"Abigail is it?" Marsh said in a lilting voice. "Wots' this I hear from Devi that you've saved us all from a deep problem?" Abigail couldn't place his accent, but took his meaning clear enough.

"Well," she started, taking another much smaller sip from her bottle. "It was nothing much really. A drift in the magnetic resonance of one of your Tesla engines. Chief Neelam, I mean Devi, would have dealt with it fine. I simply happened to have a tool to make re-balancing easier." The old man looked at her with new respect.

"You could re-balance the resonance while the engine was running?" Bobby remarked in wonder. He shook his head at the thought. "I be thinking that it was more than simple, my sister."

"Not at all," Abigail said to him easily. Because she found talking of herself uncomfortable she changed the subject. "Please forgive my ignorance, as I know little of airships," she said, "but what do you do as 'Chief Rigger'? I know of the term from sailing ships, but we have no sails." A wide smile again split the black face.

"Well, riggers mostly work on the open spaces of the upper hull," he explained. "We patch leaks in the gas cells, fix the wiring, handle the cargo, and go topside when it's needed, course."

"Topside?" Abigail asked curiously.

"He means they go outside on the top of the ship while we're in flight," Will explained to her.

"Oh," Abigail said, in a subdued voice. She could imagine how dangerous such a thing would be flying thousands of feet above the ground. "That must require very strong nerves," she observed. Bobby shrugged.

"It no happen that often," he said, "exceptin' when we gets in fights. Then we have holes to patch, or the damn running lights to fix. They are always gettin' shot up." He tipped his bottle up to his lips, then grinned at her.

"Besides is nothing like it in all the world," he said still grinning. "You are walkin' in the clouds like a god. I will take you out on the ship sometime if you like."

"Forgive me for asking, Lady Abigail," Naomi said from across the table, "but I don't know much about Tesla engines. Drift of what resonance?" Abigail looked at the woman.

"Just Abigail, please," she said with a smile. "You know how Tesla engines work yes?"

"Sort of," the woman replied, "something about how the ball inside takes energy from the earth, correct?" Abigail nodded. The young woman had a better understanding than many she had been to a party with.

"Essentially, yes," Abigail agreed. "The 'ball' is really a series of special loops suspended in a magnetic fluid that is tuned to the same Aetherwave' as the earth herself generates," she explained. "The loops *capture* this energy and spin with what they've captured in a magnetically induced tension. We then..."

"Use that energy as electricity," McGuire finished for her.

"Yes, essentially," Abigail acknowledged, while trying not to be annoyed at the redheads' interruption. "Sometimes the magnetic resonance of the loops 'slip' for lack of a better word, in relation to each other, we really don't know why. When that happens the electricity generated begins to oscillate, spiking and then falling. Then we must realign all the loops magnetic resonance such that they flow smoothly again."

"What happens when you don't do that?" Naomi asked, sipping at her drink.

"The engine goes boom in a most spectacular fashion, it does," McGuire said taking a large swig from his bottle. "And takes yon ship with it more often than not," he set his bottle back down with a thump.

"That can happen," Abigail allowed. "Although it's usual to take the engine off line before matters reach that far." She looked at the operator over her bottle mouth. "Are you interested in Energetics, Mr. McGuire?" He shrugged, taking another deep pull from his bottle.

"I've learned a bit here an' there," he said shortly. "Are you interested that your fancy title comes from stealing the food of starving Irish children, Lady Hadley?"

"McGuire," Saira hissed, "the woman is a guest, and has done us a good turn of her own will, as well." Abigail blinked, and looked from Saira back to McGuire. She narrowed her eyes at McGuire.

"I'm afraid that I don't know what you mean by that statement, Mr. McGuire," Abigail replied coldly. "I have never stolen food from anyone."

"Is that so?" McGuire challenged, "But you still uphold and serve the Famine Queen don't you? The self-same one who tried to turn back the food ships in '40, and then dragooned the men of Ireland in '77 at bayonet point to be grist for the Invaders? There be a lot of blood on that throne you take your title from Lady Hadley."

Abigail looked around the table. Most of the faces where blank, Will returned her look with an up raised eyebrow as if interested in her reply. Saira looked as if she could kill McGuire. She would receive no help there. Abigail turned her gaze back to the Irishman.

"First of all, Mr. McGuire," she began tartly, "I'm afraid that I know very little about the famine of 1840, although from what I have read, I believe that there was incompetence and error on both sides of the sea. As for the events of '77, I have only second hand knowledge of those. With my mother dead, and my father aiding the science effort, I was at the Blackpool Relocation Camp."

There was a moment of silence at this revelation. Blackpool had become infamous for its horrible conditions during the war. Starvation and corruption were only the start of it. It was talked about that nearly as many people had died in the relocation camps as had been killed by the Invaders.

"Although," Abigail continued, "if what I have heard of the Irish brigades is even half true, they surely fought as magnificently as they could drink," she paused to drink from her own bottle. "Which, if you are any example," she continued, "must have been truly magnificent indeed." Low chuckles from around the table greeted this.

"Finally, "Abigail continued with some force, "Her Majesty Queen Victoria made possible the gathering of the Savants who, led by Dr. Tesla, created the science that defeated the Invaders in Britain. Then she gave that knowledge to the whole world so that everyone might defend themselves against the invader's depredations, rather than hoard it exclusively for the Empire." She made a great show of looking around the airship mess hall.

"A fact which I believe means that without Her Majesty's good rule we would not be here having this discussion. And which I also believe you yourself just acknowledged in the toast Will gave." She took another drink from her bottle and set it down looking at McGuire in challenge.

The table burst into spontaneous applause at her conclusion while McGuire had been getting increasingly red faced at her lecture. He threw back his head and howled in approval while slapping the table.

"I will say this for ye, girl," he gasped. "You've got some brass ones that's for sure and all!" Finding his bottle empty, he waved it in the air signaling that he wanted another. "But surely being an intelligent person, can you not agree that..." He was interrupted by Devi Neelam coming up to the table.

She was barefoot, and dressed in a flowing robe of a deep blue that Abigail knew was called a sari.

"Paddy McGuire," she scolded him. "Do not be telling me that you have been haranguing Lady Hadley with your politics after she has worked for days to save your worthless posterior!"

"Now Devi," McGuire pleaded, raising both hands as if to ward off a blow, "I was just exchanging views with our distinguished guest is all."

"It's all right, Devi," Naomi said to her. "Paddy here was just going to apologize, weren't you Michael?" The woman followed this with another poke in McGuire's side. McGuire opened his mouth working it as a fish might, then closed his jaw with a great sigh.

"Truly Lady Hadley, if my...impassioned discourse has given you any offense, I do apologize," he said drunkenly. He even sounded sincere.

"Accepted Mr. McGuire, we need speak of it no further," Abigail replied in the ritual words that said they would not go to dueling over what had been said. Dueling had become very popular since the War. Even Her Majesty, Victoria, approved of it in certain circumstances.

McGuire's eyes widened at the ritual phrasing that indicated that there would be no duel over the conversation. Clearly, he hadn't considered that she might actually call him out over what he had said. She smiled at his astonishment.

"And please, call me Abigail at this time," she finished sweetly with a smile.

"Indeed, then let us speak of it no further," he smiled back as he gave her the ritualistic dueling response, indicating that the matter was finished between them while acknowledging his wrong. "And I'd be pleased if you'd call me Paddy at this time, for I'm surely drunk."

Another bottle was slapped down on the table at his elbow. He went to open it, and announced to the table in general, "Damn me, but I think I like her."

Devi, still standing at the end of the table, gave an aristocratic snort at this pronouncement and turned to Saira.

"Are you ready to go?" she asked. Saira looked at Jarro, who nodded. She leapt up from Jarro's lap. The helmsman followed her in standing. The first thing that Abigail could see was that he was very tall.

"Ready and more than," Saira said gratefully. "Politics gives me a rash." She removed her robe, followed by the man, Jarro. Both of them were naked save for something like a loincloth, their skin gleaming with oil. Saira also had a band of cloth restraining her ample breasts, a necklace of old silver around her throat. Seeing Abigail's look of surprise, she gave a saucy wink at her.

"Enjoy the show," she said, and swayed off towards the stage. The crew, seeing the pair, began to call out encouragement. The table pounding resumed building in a rhythm that drowned out everything else. Abigail shot a look of inquiry at Will, wondering what she was about to see. He smiled, pointing at the stage, "Watch," he said.

Suddenly, the electric tubes went dark, leaving the room illuminated only by the flickering light of the gas mantles along the walls. The table pounding cut off as suddenly. A few notes from Devi's stringed instrument sounded as Saira entered the center of the cleared space. Her pantomime appeared as graceful as any ballerina that Abigail had even seen. Saira was a hunter, weary from the hunt, the spear she mimed leaning against seemed almost real to Abigail as she watched. A flute took up a winding harmony as Saira stretched, looked about to see there was no danger, and then gracefully sank to the ground in mock slumber.

A small drum began a faint snarling rhythm that grew louder as Jarro, on all fours now, stalked into the clearing. Clearly he was a lord of the beasts, powerful and cunning. Discovering the sleeping hunter, he crouched, preparing to spring. The drum was joined by another as the flute sang notes of distress. The hunter jumped up, spear held before her. The two faced off, crouching. Then accompanied by a crescendo of music, they attacked. Spinning and lunging, twirling and stabbing the two fought back and forth across the cleared space of the floor. Abigail watched, spellbound.

With a final amazing leap through the air, the hunter's spear pierced the beast, and he collapsed, with the hunter standing over him.

Silence.

Stillness.

Then the notes of a flute solo wound through the air as the hunter raised arms to the heavens as if in an offering. Slowly, a winged bird appeared to rise from the body of the beast. Jarro moved incredibly lightly for one so large. He danced, his form flying around the hunter. She lowered her arms and turned towards him, arms outstretched, trying to capture him. But the bird managed to flit away, always at the last possible moment.

The hunter followed the bird as the two danced around and around each other, skin gleaming in the gas light. Touch, whirl, touch, the music complex and plaintive, until at last, the bird opened wide his wings to the hunter. She entered his embrace, head flung back in surrender as the music soared. His wings enveloped her. The two, entwined as one, floated to the floor on the last note.

The silence in the room was absolute until a lone voice shouted in acclaim. The room burst into whistles, shouts, and pounding on tables and floors. Abigail, realizing that she had been holding her breath, leapt to her feet in applause. Seeing her do so, others followed until the whole room was standing.

Saira and Jarro stood hand in hand as the applause rolled over them. She said something to the man, and they executed as perfect a bow as you'd ever see on a London stage, Abigail thought. Laughter and more applause greeted this. Then Saira turned, leaping into the taller man's arms. They locked in a passionate kiss. Cat calls, and more laughter followed this display. Saira then did a backflip out of his arms, and still holding hands, the two raced out the mess doors, the acclaim of the hall following them. As Will and Abigail sat again, he turned to her smiling.

"Well, that's the last we'll see of them tonight," he predicted. He reached for one of the filled buns on the table. "Here try one of these. Wu makes 'em, and usually outdoes himself. They're called 'Dim Sum' which means 'small treasures'. "

Abigail picked up one of the buns and tried it. Hot spicy filling exploded in her mouth along with some sort of crunchy vegetables. It was really quite good.

"I see that you allow somewhat informal relations on your ship, Will," she said around another bite.

"What?" Will asked in confusion as he finished his bun. Then, catching her meaning, he shrugged. "What anyone does on their off time is their business. The main rules are no opium, nor white. No stealing or killing. No one lays a hand on anyone unwilling."

"What happens if they break those rules?" she wondered.

"If they're that stupid, they go out the hatch," he said grimly. "As for Saira, or anyone else for that matter, they can sleep with who they please." Will shrugged again, "We're not like your British high society out here Abigail." He laughed, "I'm certainly not one of your Christian captains. Who loves with who, is nobody else's damn business. No more than is what they eat for breakfast really. We're free people here. I guess that was what I was trying to say earlier."

"Oh," she replied. There really didn't seem much more to say to that. He was right in that it wasn't like 'high society' at all. It seemed that up here your accomplishments mattered more than the accident of your birth. That what you set your hand to determined who you were, what you did. In 'society' her station would allow her to be head of a College department, but not to fix Tesla engines all day long as she had been doing. That you could take pleasure with whom you wished she had to admit was a tempting thought.

In 'society' people had relations of course, but it was all very much hidden. It was understood that very few should approach the altar as an innocent, but how that happened was never talked about openly. She herself had some experience, but it was always with careful consideration. The removal of pregnancy as an issue may have come with the diaphragm, but other restraints were very present. God forbid, for example, that you take a lover outside your station, or have one publicly.

The very idea that she could simply go off with someone, under her own name, and no one would do more than wish them a happy time was very liberating to contemplate. Not that she would, of course. Saira, damn her, had it too right. She was in strange waters, and the last thing she needed was to risk complicating things more. Besides, this was not some pleasure cruise, she reminded herself. She had a purpose, a duty to her father, to the world.

Still, she admired what they seemed to have won for themselves. She was under no illusions about it all. She had seen and heard enough to know that their way of life could be brutal and short, with no fixed home, always wandering. Still, she wondered if they truly appreciated what they had.

# Chapter Eleven

## Mess, Wind Dancer, South China Sea

While she engaged in these thoughts, the musicians struck up another tune. Naomi stood up from the table with a cry of "That's my song!" She strode to the front and was soon leading the room in a popular beer-hall song that was both ribald and hilarious. Abigail found herself singing along with everyone else. Will turned out to have a surprisingly good voice.

The evening followed on with more singing, dancing and even some surprisingly good poetry from a young oriental man. Abigail found that she had perhaps had more of the potent rum than she should. She'd barely finished one little bottle and found her head swimming. She reached for another of the delicious little buns to help soak up the alcohol in her belly.

As the evening wound down, more people left, in ones, twos and threes. Each stopped to give a good night to Will and those at the table. Devi was meandering through a pleasant tune on her many-stringed instrument softly, when 'Paddy' McGuire returned to his earlier topic.

"So, Abigail, as an intelligent woman, can you not see that the governing o' the Empire must be changed from its corrupt ways?" he asked. The line of empty bottles in front of him seemed not to slow down him down in the least.

"What exactly do you mean? Abigail asked warily.

"Don't get him going," Naomi pleaded with a roll of her eyes.

"What do I mean?" McGuire straightened up in his seat. Naomi waved her hands helplessly. "What do I mean?" He repeated, more loudly. "Why the un-just and decadent system of the aristocracy of course! The tyranny of absent landlords who amass wealth and privilege on the backs of common folk, saving your presence of course. The bald fact a man will be held down in his place by a silk stocking rather than rise to be whatever he can make of himself. That's what I mean!"

"But I thought we'd already agreed that Her Majesty has done many a service to all humanity, did we not?" Abigail replied. McGuire reluctantly nodded. "That, you see, is the essence of what title means, to serve your people," she said empathizing each word as she spoke it. Abigail paused as if gathering her thoughts before continuing.

"I'm afraid that you cannot condemn on one hand, and then praise on the other," she pointed out. "The decisions Her Majesty made were as much a part of the 'system' you so loudly decry as any other virtue. Certainly, there are members of the nobility that are asses. I know more than a few. Yet any numbers of them also have their titles by dint of accomplishment and hard work.

"Must there be reforms? I agree, absolutely," she nodded briskly. "The water tithe, the long hours and low wages of the resettled workers, the Star Court for the nobility and the Bailey for the other classes, the tyranny of the Colonial Officers, all are barbarisms from the War. Yes, I say again, all these and more are due to be changed."

"Should any man, or woman be allowed to make of themselves what they will? Absolutely." Abigail said in answer to her own question. "And that is starting to be true with the merit reforms. Take myself for example; I hold my own title by the sweat of my intellect, as does my father before me. And who, Mr. McGuire is leading these reforms you may ask? Why Lord Darwin, Lady Churchill, even the Crown-Princess," she said, gasping in mock horror. "Not to mention the New Party of Parliament," she said continuing. "I believe that you'll find that a good number of 'decadent aristocrats' vote New Party. I can tell you that I do. What would you have instead? A republic of some sort like the French tried?"

"Aye. That I would!" McGuire retorted. "One man, one vote! And leaders that are beholden to the people that elect them! You may talk of Parliament, but all of Ireland has not a tenth of the seats it should in the Commons, and no Irishman sit in the Lords at all! Where is our voice? You talk of noble lords and ladies, and I do grant you that there are some as seem to have their hearts in the right place. But why should we be dependin' on their hearts at all?" He finally paused for breath.

"One woman," Abigail said into the pause.

"What?" McGuire looked nonplussed.

"'One man, one woman, one vote' that is the full quote you know," Abigail said archly.

"Oh Aye," McGuire said, "I'll give ye that, one woman as well. But a republic would have such power as only was given it. And then no man, nor woman, would be in a place to draw the tyrant's mantle about them."

"Truly? That has worked so well hasn't it?" Abigail responded with false brightness. "Would you prefer the 'Republic' of Franco-Mexico with its Emperor and no vote? Or perhaps one of the American States, The Confederation for example? Oh, wait, you must be male and a landowner to vote there. You likely have your slaves take you to a poll there," she said with a barely suppressed sneer in her voice. "How about the Union of American States? Oh, so sorry it used to be bigger did it not? But with no aristocracy to hold it together, it's much smaller now, not that you don't still need the patronage of a Boss or an Industrialist to stand for office I am told. I'm sure they have no tyranny problem." She paused to take another drink. Will laughed, and pounded the table in approval of Abagail's words.

"I think Paddy that you might just be out-gunned on this one," Will observed. "As my people said to Custer at Blake's Ford, 'ready to surrender now'?" McGuire focused on the Captain blearily, in drunken offense.

"Never, you heathen!" The Irishman said, pounding the table angrily. "I tell ye, Republicanism is the way o the future! Once everyone has an Aetherwave, then those we elect will have to do as we the people direct them to do, now won't they? As for your examples, Lady Abigail, well, that's the reason that an Irish republic will be the first real success! After all, we were doing it long before your King William crossed the Channel, we were."

"Do you seriously believe that millions of people on the Aetherwave will be able to decide on anything?" Abigail asked astonished.

"Course they will," McGuire said confidently. Abigail shook her head.

"And what if there's a true emergency?" Abigail asked. "What then? For example, say that the Invaders return?"

McGuire snorted aloud at this.

"That's a weak argument and you know it," he said. "They've been looking at Mars though every telescope since the war, and have seen nothing. No lights, maybe some ruins, that's all. We killed the last of them we did." Abigail shook her head at his answer.

"We really don't know that now do we?" She returned.

"What? Don't be daft!" McGuire sputtered.

"Not at all, "Abigail said calmly. "There are many mysteries still about them. Not one single body of an Invader was ever recovered, anywhere. By all accounts, they destroyed themselves and their machinery rather than be taken at the end. They are a cipher to us still.

To cite another mystery, how is it that a race as advanced and powerful as to fly across the great gulf between the worlds could only land by crashing into the ground? I doubt that you would accept such landings." This was greeted by chuckles around the table. "For that matter," Abigail continued, "why did they have no airships of their own?" Frowns greeted her around the table at this pronouncement. Naomi spoke up for the first time.

"My father always said it was because we never gave them time to build airships," she said hesitantly. "That those great spider- walker things were all they had time to build."

"Come to that," Will mused, frowning in thought, "it did seem like they never really got what we were doing flying around them." Seeing Abigail's astonished look, he grinned at her. "I was rat catcher for my father in the old First Expeditionary, and saw more than my share of the War as a youn'un. No," he said firmly, "I think that they were doing some kind of counting coup."

"Counting what?" Abigail asked, "I am unfamiliar with that term."

"Custom of some of the plains peoples in North America. Instead of riding to war with a spear or gun, you have a stick. You ride up to the enemy and hit them lightly on the arm with it. You gain honor by showing how skilled you are."

"I would think that killing most of Western Europe, much of Britain, India, and the Americas, not to mention devastating large swaths of the planet as more than a tap on the arm," Abigail retorted. Will shrugged, holding up his hands in defense.

"Hey, they were Invaders! You said yourself that we really don't know all that much about them, even though they nearly exterminated us," he said. "I don' know, maybe we just didn't know how the game was to be played. Once they showed that they could kill as many of us as they wanted, maybe we were supposed to stop fighting. Instead, we kept on fighting, fighting until we killed all of them instead. Maybe we were not good interplanetary gentlemen." He raised his bottle to his lips.

Abigail nodded, with a new look of respect in her eyes.

"Lord Hadley, my father," she said, "has some thoughts that are very similar." Abigail stopped herself before she said anything else. She found herself blinking back tears. Too much rum, she decided. She had to change the subject. "We've yet to hear what you think, Will. Surely as a captain you can see the wisdom of having a strong single voice in a time of emergency. You rule a ship, the monarchy rules a nation."

Everyone laughed at that. Abigail looked confused as she gazed about the table.

"What did I say?" She asked them. Will smiled at her.

"Not the same thing at all," he said. "First of all, I don't 'rule' the ship, I am Captain of a free airship. They follow me because I'm good at what I do. They trust that I won't get them killed for no reason; I trust that they won't do the same to me."

"And don't forget that you bring more money our way than honest work ever could," McGuire laughed. Naomi gave him an elbow in the ribs. Will nodded.

"It's true, I do," Hunting Owl said seriously. "I don't force any of them to do anything they don't want to. Sure, once they sign the Articles, they agree that my word is law. When we are in the midst of it, there is no time for debate, and everyone does what I say. If they don't like how I want things later, they can collect their share and leave at any port. Nations don't do that."

"And if we are going back to politics we are going to say good night," Naomi announced pulling McGuire up with her by the elbow. McGuire grinned at her as he came to his feet swaying.

"Your cabin or mine darlin'?" he said in what Abigail was sure he thought was a seductive voice. She could tell from the expression on Naomi's face how seductive she thought it was.

"I am putting you to bed in your own cabin, alone," Naomi grunted while getting his arm around her shoulder. "You are drunk enough that you will start singing those mournful songs of yours."

"They're not mournful, lass," he said plaintively. "I simply want to share the heart of my homeland with you."

"Mournful." She said firmly. "Besides, we both have watch tomorrow."

"Need help there, Naomi?" Will asked standing. The bridge talker shook her head.

"It's alright, I've got the big fool," she said easily. "Night Lady Abigail, Cap'n." McGuire's head flopped over to look at Abigail.

"A most charmin' discourse Abigail, I hope that we have more. One question though, if I might." He held up a drunken index finger.

"What would that be Paddy?" Abigail asked him warily.

"Givin' what you say to be true, where did the Invaders come from, and what did they want?" He asked, suddenly earnest. Abigail looked sadly at him. She told him the truth.

"We don't know Paddy, and we may never know," she said softly. "It is science's purpose to ask questions that we do not know the answer to in the hopes that we may learn the answers." To her surprise, McGuire nodded in satisfaction, at this.

"Good," he said sounding pleased. "Then ye don't claim to be knowin' everything. I look forward to talking more."

"As do I Mr. McGuire," Abigail said. She smiled at the young woman holding him up. "Naomi, a pleasure to meet you." The woman nodded at her in leave-taking. The two made their way towards the door, with McGuire beginning a drunken croon about someone called Anachie Gordon. Will and Abigail sat back down at the now empty table. Bobby Marsh, the Chief Rigger, had stolen away while Abigail was talking to McGuire and Walters.

"He's a good man," Will said to her, "and a top form wave operator. He just gets a touch...obsessed when he's been drinking. That he likes you is a complement. you know. If you'd told him last week that he'd be drinking with a British Lady, I'm sure he'd have told you were mad." Will said with a grin.

"I like people of principle, which he certainly appears to be. Even when I think he is wrong." Abigail smiled back. "I enjoy a good debate. You should see some of the ones that we have at Cambridge. The rectors have had to ban duels by research fellows or there won't be any of us left." Will smiled at that.

"I can just see you challenging someone over a point of theory. " His dark face assumed a haughty expression as he drawled, 'I say, copper is the best conductor, pistols at dawn sir'! " He shook his fist in a passable imitation of an upper-crust figure. Abigail laughed, visualizing some of her fellow Scholars behaving similarly.

"Well, it isn't quite that bad, but close enough," She allowed. She frowned and then went silent.

'What are you thinking?" He gently asked her after a moment. She had the presence to look abashed as she looked at him.

"Oh, I..." gathering her breath, she spoke in a hurry as if afraid she would change her mind. "May I ask you what may be an impertinent question?"

'If you don't mind an impertinent answer, go ahead," Will replied easily.

"Why do you do what you do?" she asked hesitantly. "I saw the aftermath of the battle on the ship. I was sure that I had fallen in with another bloody-handed lot of killers. But seeing this," she pointed at the dais, "and talking with you, Saira, Devi and Paddy, I wonder why you do it? You are certainly intelligent. Why don't you just trade cargoes or something? Why not let the navies do the fighting?"

Will hesitated. He knew that he'd had too much to drink, and needed to gather his thoughts. He used the time to fill and light his pipe with a Lucifer stick, before answering her.

"We are a lot of bloody-handed killers, Abigail," he smiled thinly at her as the smoke rolled out between her lips. "That is what we do. We don't kill for no reason, and we don't kill just because some deep pocket gives us money to kill someone. We generally don't kill at all unless they try to kill us first, but it is what we do, make no mistake." He puffed on the pipe stem for a few moments, the smoke wreathing him in a gray shroud. "We're good at it too; for all that we mostly take no pleasure in it." He drew on the pipe again, before continuing.

"As for why, everyone has their own reasons. Mostly though, I like to think that it's because of what I said. We're all mongrels in one way or another on the Dancer, and deep down we can't abide those who are just plain mean to them what is weaker." He waved his pipe. "I give you one Hu Fan, a rabid dog, bringing misery and death because he liked it." He replaced his pipe and drew on it some more, "And then there are those who do it 'cause they think they got a right to. Which is most righteous feeling sorts, including your governments, in my opinion, to answer your earlier question."

"I am sorry, but I do not follow you there," Abigail frowned.

Will spread his hands in opening gestures while he talked.

"I've traveled around a fair bit, and seen a bit more, Abigail," he explained. "Mostly from where I stand, a 'government' no matter the names, or customs, comes down to a man with a gun at your head telling you what he wants you to do, or not do, for your own good. Most bandits are more honest at least." He shook his head, "I don't think that's how we were meant to live."

"I think that is a bit over simple," Abigail said curious now, "but given that, how are we supposed to live then?"

"We are meant to be Free." Will said simply. "We should live so that we can follow the spirit of our hearts." He looked at her, "You still don't understand." He stood up, holding out his hand, "Come with me and I'll show you something that may help explain it."

Abagail regarded his hand before taking it. From another man at another time, she might have taken this as an invitation to ending the evening in bed, to put it delicately. However, she had observed that while the Wind Dancer's crew were physically demonstrative, they were also refreshingly direct in their intentions.  Captain Will had given her no indications of any such intent.

Therefore, she took his offered hand without further reservations, and the two of them walked out of the mess together, nodding to Devi as they went. She nodded back briefly, then returned to her music, the Engineers' face awash in a serenity that Abigail envied.

Wordlessly, Will took them up a winding wood stair, them down the corridor to a wooden cage set in the wall. Abigail recognized that it was some type of lift.

"Where are we going?" Abigail asked.

"Topside crow's nest," he replied. "Been there yet?"

"No, I haven't," Abigail replied in puzzlement. Will grinned at her.

"Thought not," He gripped a lever set on a pedestal. "Not afraid of heights are you?"

"Not as such, no," Abigail answered. There was a whine and the sudden sensation of motion, as Will pulled the lever.

They emerged into a large open space that she thought was many yards across, though it was difficult to tell as the only illumination came from faint rows of light tubes that stretched horizontally before and behind her. As a figure passed before one of the lights, she realized that they marked walkways that ran the length of the upper hull.

"We're following a shaft that goes though the center of the main hull," Will explained. "Mostly it's so that we can get supplies up to Bobby and his riggers if there's a large enough leak in one of the gas cells or the like."

"But this is amazing," she exclaimed, Brushing back a loose strand of hair. She looked back at Will excitedly. "I had read that airships must by their construction have a large open space in the upper hull, but I had no idea it was so, well, enormous." Will grinned at her.

"Something, isn't it?" He looked around. "Mostly how big the space is becomes a balancing act. The space has to offset the weight of the occupied levels minus the number and size of lift gas cells." He gave a one shoulder shrug, "I like to keep Dancer light and frisky, and so we always run a few tons under budget."

Abigail nodded understanding, while crossing her arms against the increasing chill as they rose. She didn't imagine they could heat such a large area in any practical way. In fact, the heating and cooling of the air itself must be one of those factors in the Captain's 'balancing act'. Everything would have to be considered, she thought in approval. It was very scientific really. This led her to another revelation.

"Of course," she said animatedly, "That is also why everything aboard that can be made of wood or cloth is, because of the weight factor." Will leaned back against the wooden cage with his arms crossed, smiling at her enthusiasm. It was good to see her perk up.

"Aiya," he agreed easily. "We're not at strict about it as say, a merchant ship is, but that's the general idea. Like I said, I like to run her light so there's more room for unexpected cargo such as British Scholars."

Abigail didn't quite know what to make of that last. Her eyes narrowed, as she realized he was dissembling somewhat. She looked at him as if taking his measure all over again. It took a certain intellect to be able to effectively run such an enterprise, and from what she had seen William Hunting Owl was very effective at it. She tilted her head, regarding him. A sharp noxious odor suddenly assailed her nose.

"I say," she remarked, "What is that odor? That can't be a good thing."

"Lift gas," Will pronounced. He looked unperturbed. "There's always some lift gas that escapes into the main cavity, no matter how good your maintenance is. We must be going through a small cloud of it."

"They add something to it that makes it smell bad so that it's easier to find a leak, you know. It's nothing to worry about, it won't kill you, but it may make you talk funny for a minute if it gets strong enough in concentration."

"Yes, I'm familiar with the effect," Abigail smiled in memory at this. "We used to inhale lift gas mixtures in school to change our voices. We thought it quite the lark." She placed a hand over her nose. "It didn't smell anything like this however."

"You get used to it," he said wistfully. "Back when my Da was on the John Paul, all of us ratcatchers would sneak up into the cavity together, and poke a hole in a lift cell with a metal straw to do the same thing." He looked up, "Good. We're here."

Abigail looked up to see a hole the ceiling from which light poured down. The cage was moving up through it and then came to a shuddering halt in some sort of room. Abigail had to blink for a moment in the relative brightness, after the darkness of their ascent.

The room was lined with many portholes, broken up by heavy coats and other equipment on hooks. In the center stood another of those corkscrew stairwells the ship seemed to favor, leading up. Will walked over to it and leant against the railing. He looked up the stairway.

"Ahoy the nest!' he called. A startled white face peered down at them though the opening.

"Ahoy Cap'n!' the man greeted. "All's quiet as far as we can see."

"Good John, good," Will grinned up at him, "Just wanted to wish you a good Second Day. Sorry you drew the watch, it was a good party. The Lady Abigail and I are just going to go outside for a bit."

"Short end of the straw Cap'n," the man replied easily. "Tell me that we'll get shore-leave this landing though."

"Can't promise you that", Will shook his head. "Depends on how well the business goes."

"We rightly should you know, after missing the last two ports o call." John replied. "Ain't fair is what it is."

"I'll see what I can do, John," Will promised. "You'll be on the first call if leave happens."

"Can't ask for more than that," he said in satisfied tones. "We'll get back to it then, if there's nothing else, Cap'n." Will waved him away.

"Carry on John," he said. "We'll show ourselves out when we're done."

"Aye, aye Cap'n. Enjoy, it's a fine night." The face vanished. Will walked over to a wall. He picked up two of the heavy coats, handing one to Abigail.

"You might want to put this on," Will advised. "It does get chilly outside."

"Are we going outside?' Abigail asked, taking the coat.

"Downstairs you asked why we do this," he said earnestly. I want to show you something. Indulge me?" He held open the door for her. The sudden change of air pressure moved her hair. She glanced at him uncertainly, then stepped through the door.

Abigail nearly stumbled. They were on a narrow platform with a wooden railing. In the clear night air all she could see about her were stars. It was as if she were swimming through the void itself. She clutched the railing reflexively. She heard the door close behind her, and then Will's voice was at her ear.

"It gets everyone that way the first time," he moved carefully around her. "Keep hold of the rail and follow me." She followed behind him. At the front of the enclosed 'crow's nest' he stopped. There was room enough for her to stand beside him on the platform. What she assumed was a mount for either a telescope or a weapon of some kind was fixed to the railing between them.

Will swept his arm outward silently. She looked at the view before her; it was breath-taking in its beauty. Gleaming sliver in the moonlight, the top of the giant ship was like a sea prow moving through an ocean of stars. Except for the wind and the deep far away drone of the distant propellers, it was surprisingly silent. She breathed deeply of the cold air, and realized that no matter how clean the ship and crew where, there was a pervasive odor of 'person' for lack of a better descriptor, that she had simply blocked out of her awareness. It was gone from her nose for the first time in days. She breathed again, marveling at the view before her. They stood that way together in silence for some time. Finally Will spoke almost too softly for her to hear over the wind.

"You asked why we do what we do," he said quietly. "This is the real why. So we can keep doing this. Do you see any empires, or kings, or presidents up here? This," his arm moved in an arc over his head, "this is where Man was meant to be and what he was meant to be doing." He looked at Abigail and gave her a half salute. "And Woman too of course". She nodded silently and together they looked out at the passage of the stars around them.

After a time in the silence, he spoke again.

"Thing is," he said low enough that she had to focus her attention to hear him, "there are people aplenty who don't want us to have this. They'd rather hold us down under them, just to do it, you know. They'd rather kill everything and everyone that's is good for mere greed, than let anyone have something that they might not be able to grasp."

"The why of it don't really matter, in my opinion." He said with a shrug. "Some do it because they think that the color of their skin makes them better than others. Same thing except it's because of what lies between their legs, the Spirits they sing to, or the tongue they grew up speaking."

"But not everyone is like that," Abigail protested. "Even those who are like that, mostly are that way because of their sincere beliefs, however mistaken."

"I don't know about that," Will retorted. "I think it's mostly because they're afraid of something, and then they make up reasons why. But that's not my call, you see. I don't claim to know what's better for them, even when they claim they do know what's better for me."

"They're wrong, Lady Hadley," Will went on. "I know what's for me, and it's this," he said pointing into the sky. "I'll fight to keep it, and I'll fight anybody who tries to keep anyone else from it too if this is what they want. No matter how noble their words are, you know, at the end of the day, they're just small and mean to deny anyone this. We were meant to walk in Beauty, Lady Hadley, We were meant to fly."

Abigail looked at his head framed against the stars, and found there was nothing she could say to that. She found that his words had touched something deep in her heart, even as her mind turned them over and over. She looked back out at the universe, and felt both exalted and small at the same time. She thought of her own life, and what had brought her to this place. Impulsively she asked him without turning away from the stars before them.

"Captain, if you could have the power to do anything, anything at all, what would you do with it?" She felt him to turn to look at her puzzled by the question.

"What kind of power?" He asked. "Do you mean wave-your-hands-poof spook-type power, or engine power, or 'the world has to be as I want' power?"

"More like engine power. But with it you could potentially do everything you just listed," she said. Will looked out at the stars in thought for a while.

"I would do what your Queen Victoria did twenty-five years ago," he finally answered her. "I would give it to everyone."

"But the whole human race was facing extinction then!" She objected turning towards him. "The world isn't like that now. As you just said, there are rabid people and people who want to 'hold others down' because they can. Assume this power could give them the means to do that, or destroy everything, even themselves. Do you really think that it should be handed over to them? Wouldn't it be better to have wise and benevolent people use it for the good of everyone?" Will audibly blew out his breath at this before he answered her.

"Well, not having met anyone like you just described, who's that wise and that benevolent and all, I couldn't say really," he said slowly. "The rest of us haven't done that well with what we have now you could say, but I surely do like it that we all have it, more or less." He looked up at the stars and then grinned at her. "Maybe you would still need people like us around to deal with the mean ones."

She turned from him and back to looking at the stars.

"Perhaps we would," she breathed. For the first time, her heart whispered that maybe, just maybe, she was wrong. The honest scientific mind set she had worked so hard to hone would not allow her to avoid the conclusion that by extension, so was her father and the others of the scientific Cabal. Was it really that they were being responsible? Or were they perhaps being 'small and mean' to limit the knowledge of such power to only themselves? She suspected how the Captain and the others of Wind Dancer would view the Cabal and it goals. At best, 'arrogant bunch of toffs' came to mind. She found that she did not care for that view. No, she did not care for it at all.

"I can tell you what I would do with that kind of power myself, though," Will said, interrupting her dark thoughts. She turned her attention back to him curious as to his answer.

"Oh, and what would that be?" She asked him

"I would want to fly up there, and touch them," he said, pointing up at the stars. They both gazed up at the stars for some time in silence. Finally, she looked over at him.

"Thank you Captain," Abigail said. "I think perhaps I understand, a little at least, what you mean. May we go in now? It's quite cold."

"Of course," Will said. "It gets that way at seven hundred feet, even in the warm latitudes." They returned the coats to their hooks and after bidding the lookout a good evening, they descended in the lift in silence. As the lift slowed towards their level Will turned towards her.

"So we'll be docking in Hong Kong day after, well, today really," he remarked. "I imagine you'll be glad to get on with your father."

"Yes," she smiled, "I will." The lift stopped and they both got out. Will pointed the way they were to go, seeing that Lady Hadley was momentarily disoriented. They walked along side by side quietly towards her cabin.

"What is it that you and he are doing again?" Will asked finally as they neared her cabin door. Abigail did not even pretend not to understand his question. Instead she gave him the cover story that her father and she had agreed on before he had left on his current expedition.

That her father had been searching for the methods of the Invaders power generation was hardly secret among their peers. He, and later both of them, had been searching for years for an intact power system that the mysterious Invaders had used, haunting old War sites throughout Europe. They had discovered some interesting artifacts, and published not a few interesting theoretical articles as they sought to re-create what the Invaders had used. So thorough, however, had the Invaders been in the destruction of their equipment that the Hadley's hunting had been unsuccessful.

When an underground movement called the Science Cabal had contacted the Hadley family with an offer of aid to further their discoveries they had joined it freely. The Cabal's avowed aims of creating a scientific group of world rulers did not seem very different than what some of the New Party had advocated, only more silent in its efforts. Besides, the addition in funds had enabled Lord Hadley to investigate promising sites around the world. Abigail had remained in New Oxford, performing the duties required of them both as members of the Royal Order of Scholars. His expeditions were not exactly illegal, merely unconventional.

The coded Aetherwave message Lord Hadley had sent to her from Hong Kong had prompted Abigail to begin this secret madcap adventure of her own in order to aid him. They had estimated that the Invaders were able to call upon energy generation in limitless quantities. The discovery of an intact Invader power source would shake not only the international scientific community, but the entire world order, they had both been sure. That they had decided not to tell the British government, let alone their fellow Scholars in the Cabal, now began to seem to Abigail as perhaps not so wise. However, she said none of this she said to the Captain.

"We're surveying how the power distribution could be improved," she replied not looking at him. Lying to this man did not feel right somehow, despite everything.

Will nodded, saying nothing for a moment. Even his grandmother wouldn't have bought that one, he thought. So, she was lying because she had a secret. That was alright, he thought. He knew something about having secrets. He had a few of his own. He'd just hoped that maybe she'd tell him hers. She hadn't. That didn't mean that their secrets were at cross purposes. Maybe they weren't he thought hopefully. Only time would tell if it was a vain hope or a true one. Still, the hunt must go on.

"That's right," He said to her easily. "You did mention something about that, now I recall. Well, from what I've seen of China that could help a lot of people. End a lot of misery." They had reached her cabin door.

"Yes," she smiled at him, "That's as science should do you know." She paused, as if deciding what to say, and then spoke again, "Well Captain Hunting Owl, thank you for a most wonderful evening. If I may say so, your crew, and yourself, are really most extraordinary." Will gave her his grin and touched his finger to forehead in salute.

"We aim to please, Lady Hadley," he said and turned to go. She began to do the same, then impulsively turned back towards him.

"My friends call me Abigail. I do hope that we may be friends, Captain." She faltered a moment. not sure what she was asking. "That is, if you wish."

He grinned again, folding his arms across his chest.

"Well Abigail, in that case, then you should call me Will, and yes we surely may, and yes I would."

She nodded and faintly smiled back.

"Alright then. Goodnight, Will." She turned to go inside, but stopped when he spoke again.

"Abigail," he asked. "Can you shoot a pistol?" She turned full back towards him in astonishment. Of all the things that a handsome man might ask her at her door, she had never expected something like that.

"Yes I can," she said, "Although rapier was always my best in dueling class. Why do you ask?"

"Sword, eh?" He rubbed his chin at her answer. "I can see that. If you don't mind my asking, you ever duel for real, or anything like it, outside of this 'dueling class'?" She blinked at the change of subject, unsure as to what he was about.

"No, I haven't," she said perplexed. "But I must say, I don't intend to start any duels in China!"

"Be that as it may," he allowed. "I think that you have seen that all out here is not quite as it is back in merry old England. We have got a few spare guns. I think you should have one." She looked at him in astonishment. "What would I do with a gun?" Will looked suddenly very serious.

"Nothing, I hope." He said quietly.

"Well I should think not!" Abigail exclaimed. Then she remembered to lower her voice to match his in the corridor. "I am a Scholar after all," she said quietly, "not a...a gunsel."

"Good!" He grinned at her. "I will have Saira meet up with you at mid watch then. Consult with her. You can pick out something that suits." He turned and started to walk down the corridor.

"Wait! I don't want a gun!" Abigail hissed after him.

"Sleep on it," he said over his shoulder. He waved again without breaking stride. "Good night, Abigail." He slowed when he heard her cabin door slam shut. He turned around, and looked back at the door, thumbs in his gun belt, thinking.

He hadn't intended to spring the idea on her like that, but he suddenly had a hunch, and he did not have time for her mannerly objections. At least, this way he could be sure she would think about it. He didn't know if Abigail knew that her father had been making underworld contacts, nor did he know the trouble that she might face in Hong Kong. His hunch though was that that she would welcome having a gun at some point. He had some experience with hunches.

# Chapter Twelve

## Cherry Blossom Lane, Hong Kong

Lord Albert Leighton, Royal Order of Scholars wrinkled his nose at the loathsome smells that permeated through his breathing mask as he carefully picked his way down the murky lane. Albert hated everything about Hong Kong. The smells, the foul air, the heat .It was no place for an Englishman. He cursed the day he had been foolish enough to accept a commission in the Colonial Government. Assistant director of Aetherwave Operations had sounded so much more impressive than the reality had turned out to be.

His days were spent trapped between maddening boredom and the humiliation of having to listen to that toad, White. The director was an incompetent pig. By rights, Albert should have his position, not be relegated to being little more than the office tinker. It was a bitter disappointment to him. In consolation, his nights were spent at first with gambling and drink. Gradually he moved into the more disreputable sections of the city as his debts grew and the better houses would no longer have him. Then he had discovered the pleasant dreams of what the locals called the white dragon.

At first, the opium had been his salvation. It had made even this hellish place seem survivable. Then as his time in the opium dens had grown, White's demands on him seemed to increase, even while Albert's exchequer diminished. Albert had been at the point of despair when the offer appeared wearing the face of an angel. He had seized that opportunity with both hands. It had taken courage to do so he knew, but tonight would see him free of this accursed place forever.

He startled at a noise, hand going to the handle of his sword cane. The place named for the meeting was not in an area that a white man normally would visit alone at night. He was far from afraid however. After all, he was a young man of strong constitution with experience in the Barjitsu fighting arts, learned from the master of the arts himself in London. Still, even a lion was wary of jackals. He peered through the shadows ahead of him as he inched forward. The lane was only dimly lit by a gaslight at the street corner behind him.

A small shape coalesced out of the darkness. He relaxed as a familiar voice spoke.

"Are you certain you were not followed?" The lilting voice sang out to him. Albert pulled off his breather, and smiled at the shadowy figure.

"Yes," Albert replied. "I did exactly as you requested. I came by way of both the harbor, and the air tower. I changed bishaws often. I was not followed."

The small figure came forward and a glint of gold curls shone in the dim light. She smiled up at him.

"Good, Albert. Good," she said in her lilting accent. "And have you finished your tasks?"

"Yes," the Scholar replied. "I replaced the crystals of the Governor's own wave set earlier today on a maintenance pretext. That was the last of them." He frowned at her. "You do know that they will discover the substitutions in days, a few weeks at most. I really fail to see what this accomplishes."

"That is not your concern Albert," his little Russian angel reminded him.

Albert shrugged in agreement. It really wasn't his concern. The Russians and the British had been adversaries in the Game of Empire since before the War, and still were. The principles of the once grand Alliance of Nation—to be united against the Invaders—were paid lip service to, and little more than that. Why should he care if the Russians wanted to snarl up communications in this God forsaken armpit for a few days?

She stepped closer. He was surprised to see that the tiny Russian woman was now wearing the black pants and frogged coat of the natives, rather than the corset and silks that she wore when they met. No matter. He did not really find her china-doll beauty attractive, though he could appreciate it in the abstract. He held out a bag that jiggled with crystals. He knew that discreet connection crystals such as these were worth far more than what he was being paid, but beggars could not be choosers. She took the bag from his hand.

"I've kept up my end," He said briskly. "Now where is the rest of what I am due?" It had been agreed that part of his final payment would be arrangements for him to leave Hong

Kong for wherever he wished, in addition to ten thousand pounds in negotiable bank bonds. A few days from now would find him in Jakarta, and from there a whole new life was waiting.

"Ah yes, your due," the small woman said. She was now inches away. Albert hoped that she would not attempt some sort of sordid seduction instead of paying him. He started to raise his hand to stop her.

"Really, I..." he felt a sharp coldness in his guts. His hand felt suddenly far away as blackness dropped over him.

Illiya Petrov wiped her blade on the Englishman's coat, and then stepped back, careful of the blood spray from the corpse. She breathed heavily for a moment, looking down at the body.

"Take him away," she finally ordered. Two members of a local Han gang she had subverted came out of the shadows to pick up the body.

She walked to the far end of the lane where a steam car hissed, waiting for her. She could have had the men kill him, but she had so few pleasures left of her own. Her spirit sensed with approval the fear of the Han driver who held the door open for her. It had been laughably easy to seize control of a sizable portion of the city's criminal brotherhoods, using nothing more than murder and money.

When she had first been placed in charge of Operation Jade, she have met with the smaller underworld leaders of Hong Kong to offer them what she was careful to imply was Imperial Russian aid to undermine their British overlords. The former leaders had called her the 'White Doll' at that first meeting when they thought she could not understand their language. She had enlightened them that she understood it very well, and the walls had run red with their blood. She smiled at the memory. Their successors now whispered her name as the White Death.

As soon as Kane arrived with the Hadley woman, they could begin to extend control over the older crime organizations, beginning with An Fong. Once he was subdued, the others would quickly fall in line. Now that the government Aetherwave sets were compromised, phase two could begin, and none too soon. It had been an order from the Master that they were also to deal with this Hadley affair in addition to Operation Jade. Sending Kane to capture the woman had left her short-handed. She frowned, seeing one of the local gang leaders sitting within the cabin of her car.

"Why are you here," she asked him coldly in Cantonese. The man could barely contain his terror, she noticed with contempt.

"Forgive me," he said in a rush. "Our source within the An Fong House reports that the awaited package will arrive in his hands tomorrow."

"What?" She hissed, as the man flinched. "How is that possible?" The denial of An Fong's delivery would greatly weaken the Fong House. That was the reason that Kane had been detailed to intercept it. Kane had been certain that the additional task of capturing the Hadley girl would present no great problems. Petrov had agreed with his assessment, and given him permission to proceed. That had been the last communication she had from him.

"I do not know Great Lady," the gang leader replied. "Only that it is to be delivered by a Captain Hunting Owl of the airship Wind Dancer."

Illiya snarled wordlessly and the gang leader flinched. The Wind Dancer and Hunting Owl she thought to herself. He and that half-breed bitch had been trouble enough in Cairo. She had never been satisfied with the outcome of that encounter. But, how could he know of their plans? What had happened to Kane? She gathered her thoughts, there were too many questions raised by this news.

"Was there any mention of a woman named Hadley as well?" she asked. The man shook his head rapidly more afraid than he had ever been. He had seen other men horribly killed by her for bringing bad news.

"No, Great Lady," he said desperately. "If you wish I can give orders to inquire?"

"No, you wrenched dolt! Be quiet." She thought for a moment, while the man sweated in the car across from her.

"What you will do is send men to watch the air towers," she directed. "As soon as the Wind Dancer docks I wish to know of it. Also if there appears to be an English Scholar with them I wish to know that as well. Also ready a team to take back the package before it reaches An Fong. Now go!" The man almost dived out the side door, grateful to escape with his life.

Illiya rapped on the partition to the driver's compartment. It scrolled down a hairs breadth, to reveal the driver's eyes.

"Back to the main house, as quickly as you can." The driver nodded scrolling up the screen. The car's steam valves hissed as the steam car began to lurch forward.

As the car turned onto the more crowded thoroughfare, Petrov snarled wordlessly at the streaming mass of people she could see through the window. They were all rats, she thought, mindless, teeming vermin that should be eliminated as useless.

She understood that her current mission was only to ensure the subversion of Hong Kong for the secret society of the Lux Invictus, rather than for Imperial Russia. Culling the population for the more suitable workers would have to come later, she knew, but she still wanted to simply wipe them all away. She was tired of the stink and the smells, and the mindless jabber all the vermin spoke in. Perhaps when Operation Jade was completed she could request heading up the culling as a boon for a job well done. The thought made her smile again.

That she had been chosen to spearhead Operation Jade was a singular honor, especially as she had only attained to the Second Circle of the Society in the last year. She looked down at her hands, feeling the strength and vitality that coursed through her as a result of her Transformation. Illiya had been a member of the Lux Invictus for only three years, but attaining the Transformation of the Second Circle had shown her that her superiors had recognized the devotion she held for the principles of the Society. That her devotion had resulted in the Transformation was a miracle indeed, especially for a one who had doubted in miracles not so long ago as the Russian assassin.

Illiya Petrov has been born into a serf family on the estate of the Boyar Chekov outside of Moscow. Though the old Tsar had 'freed the serfs' of the Boyars, or Lords, the War had changed many things. The new Tsar cared so little about those who had formerly been serfs that Illiya's family had been slaves in every way that mattered. No matter how hard her family worked, they were forever in debt to the Boyar. Illiya had been sold to the feared Okhranka, the secret police, when she turned thirteen to meet that year's tax obligation. After two years of training she had made her first kill. She smiled whenever she remembered him, an arrogant Cossack leader who had whimpered like a child before the end. Illiya still used the weapon she had made that first kill with, the Cossack's own kindjal, a long double edged dagger. It was still her favorite means of killing. She was very good at killing she discovered. Her superiors were delighted.

Some years later, she had a brief affair with a cello player in Moscow. She found the cello soothing, and at eighteen she had earned from the Okhranka the right to indulge some of her own whims. Unfortunately, he had prattled on annoyingly about love after a while. When she had attempted to end the affair because she was bored, he had gone on about some absurd theory he had learned in university about how the hardships of her early life made her incapable of loving others, which was absurd. The difference was that she had a talent that would let her rise above her station, a talent she enjoyed . . . killing. What had that boring fool with his soft hands known of that? He had continued to try to see her, and she had been annoyed enough at his behavior that she had finally killed him. It was the most satisfying moment of the whole dreary business for her.

It was shortly after that when she had attained the rank of Major in the Secret Police that she had learned of the Lux Invictus. It had been her mentor in the service who had brought her into the Light. The Unconquerable Light only accepted those who had shown that they were of superior human stock which her mentor confirmed. Illiya had always known she was superior. Their mission was nothing less than righting the decadent weakness that had been allowed to overtake the human race, replacing the inferior ruling classes with superior specimens, such as herself. The Society of the Invincible Light was everywhere around the world now, drawing in those true humans who would restore the natural order of things.

Under the guidance of the Great Masters Beyond, as one advanced in the Light one was granted a greater unfolding of their own natural superiority as well as a deeper connection to the wisdom of the Great Masters. Having only obtained the Second Circle, Illiya Petrov did not have the union of spirit that the Masters did with Great Masters Beyond. However, she could feel the Great Masters constantly at the back of her mind, waking and sleeping, like the rumble of thunder in the distance. She sighed, stroking the hilt of her kindjal. When she had obtained the First Circle she would be invincible, and she could hardly await that blessed day.

She already knew that she was stronger, faster, and smarter than inferior beings such as Hunting Owl and his motley crew of mongrels. They would not interfere this time as they had in Cairo, she vowed. No doubt an ambush by her local allies would be sufficient for the capture of Hunting Owl. If it also led to a loss of face for An Fan so much the better for Operation Jade. She could then see to the capture of the English Scholars herself. She had no doubt that bungler Kane had let the daughter slip through his fingers somehow. What the Master wanted with them was not her concern; the Master had simply ordered the Scholars' capture. It was therefore a priority, but not as high a priority as Operation Jade, she judged. Yes, she decided, as she leaned back in the push car seat, pleased with herself. Yes, she truly did possess a superior mind to craft such a plan. Soon she would turn that mind to the torment of the Wind Dancer's captain. If any of her gangster allies could have seen her smile, they would have paled.

# Chapter Thirteen

*Wind Dancer*, South China Sea

Abigail woke the next morning with surprisingly little after-effects from the night before, despite the alcohol. She had fallen asleep thinking about what the Captain had said to her.

When she applied her balanced scientific view to what he had said, and stopped being annoyed at how he had said it, she had to admit that the proposition held merit. She was resolved therefore to find Saira first. Not finding the Arms-Master in the mess, she learned while eating where Saira was likely to be. Abigail found she was becoming increasingly comfortable with the crew of the airship and, she liked to think, they with her. Asking directions as she went, she soon found herself outside the door of the cargo hold. She noticed that the door was propped open with a wedge of wood rather than closed, or 'dogged' as they said on the ship. Really, she reflected, why couldn't they simply say locked? She pushed through the door, careful to set the wedge again, and stopped at what she saw when she turned.

The hold was large, almost as large as the engine room filled with the smell of strange spices overlaying the usual scents of oil, ozone, and human in the rest of the ship. Along one wall were tiers with barrels and crates. The large space was lit by a single light tube that vainly attempted to banish the gloom. But it wasn't the room's size that stopped her but rather the small figure in the center of it.

Saira flowed like water about the room with a slightly curved long sword in each hand. The blades flashed occasionally as the woman spun, thrust, and tumbled across the floor, then made an impossible leap, easily soaring ten feet in the air. She came to a stop, sliding to one knee with both blades crossed over her head. She spoke without turning towards Abigail.

"Yes, Lady Hadley, what can I do for you," she asked formally, not even sounding out of breath.

It took Abigail a moment to answer her, a little surprised at her formal tone. As a swordswoman herself she could appreciate the deadly beauty of what she had just seen, even if she was unfamiliar with the style. It had easily been as stunning as the performance the previous night.

"That was truly beautiful," she breathed.

Saira flowed to her feet, twirling the swords once, and then moved towards a towel on a nearby crate. Despite the chill of the hold, she was barefoot, clad only in cotton pants and a cloth which bound her breasts.

"You are too kind," Saira said gracefully placing the swords down on the crate, and picked up the towel. "I rarely get to use the dalwar," she said indicating the swords, "and am sorely out of practice with them." She frowned, "My Raishi would not be pleased with me."

"I would have to say that was quite marvelous," Abigail said as she walked into the hold. "I am afraid that I cannot comment on the specifics of your style though. I only know the rapier." Saira grinned at her, draping the towel about her neck.

"Ah, yes," she said, "Cap'n Will mentioned that earlier. A woman with a sword is always a beautiful thing." She took back up the swords, twisting the hilt of one towards Abigail, "Would you care to dance for a bit?"

"What, now?" Abigail asked in astonishment.

The darker woman shrugged wordlessly. Abigail took the proffered sword from her, testing its weight. It was slightly heavier than what she was used to. She took a stance, tried an experimental thrust in the air. She looked closely at the shining blade, careful not to touch it. "It is a lovely weapon." She turned towards Saira, "but I am sure that I could not follow that style of yours. I would be a poor opponent." At this, Saira took up a classic fencing stance, one hand behind her back.

"Then we will follow the style you know," Saira grinned at Abigail. "But you must have mercy, as I am not proficient with it."

Abigail paused, thinking. They had no padding or masks, and live steel rather than capped foils. In a way, Saira was paying her a complement, trusting that she, Abigail, was competent enough not to injure Saira or allow Saira to injure her. Did Abigail share that same trust of Saira? Laughing, she shrugged out of her jacket, moving into the ready stance.

"En garde, Arms-Master Brighton," she said to her across the swords.

"En garde, Lady Hadley," Saira flowed into first guard, and Abigail suspected Saira had stretched the truth about the 'not proficient' part. Then there was no time for thought, as to Abigail's' exhilaration, they danced.

What seemed to her like an endless time later, they paused. She was extremely pleased to have scored a 'hit' on the last pass. Saira had only 'killed' her five times over. The dark woman was truly amazing. Saira handed her a bottle. She drank the water down thirstily. She was, she reflected, rather badly out of shape herself.

"That last was very good," Saira remarked. "Where did you learn it?' Abigail laughed, drinking some more.

"The school of desperation," Abigail answered. She mockingly extended an arm heaven wards, 'Have mercy, I am not proficient in it!' I'll learn, when you say something like that."

"But truly, I am not proficient in it," Saira protested. "You would have defeated me easily had you more practice," she replied seriously. "Your technique is very good. As for your 'school', it would seem to me that it is a very good teacher," Saira smiled at her. "How are you with a pistol?"

"Well, my teachers said I was almost as good with an electric as the sword. Not as good with chemical guns, I am afraid." Abigail said. She frowned at the other woman. "Then I assume Captain Will explained why I am here." Saira nodded, wiping her face with a towel.

"He told me what he said," the Arms-Master replied. "What do you say?" She looked at the Scholar with her piercing blue eyes. Abagail met them for a moment, then looked off across the hold as if embarrassed.

"I have thought about it a very great deal." Abigail paused, then continued in a rush. "I want a gun," she said determinedly. "An electric pistol would be best if that is possible." She turned towards Saira, a fierceness lighting her face. "I will not be caught out again," she said grimly. "I was trained in arms as every one of my station is, mostly for 'affairs of honor' you know. I never considered that I would actually need to use that training." She waved the water bottle. "I can see where I may have been mistaken."

"I know that having one would not have prevented my circumstances when you found me," she said, "but I can see times when it may. While I can hardly carry it about like you do those two small swords of yours, I want the means to defend myself at hand."

"That is very wise of you, my sister," Saira said gravely. She bent to reach for the rest of her clothing. "Let us go up to the armory and see if we can find a sparkie pistol fit for a lady warrior." She smiled, as she pulled on her tunic. "As for carrying it, I have had some ideas."

"You do? That would be interesting," Abigail said. They moved towards the door. Abigail turned to look at her suspiciously, "Would these 'ideas' be in keeping with my persona as a Lady Scholar?" Saira flashed her white teeth, placing a hand on Abigail's back.

"Oh, I doubt it very much," the Arms-Master said brightly.

# Chapter Fourteen

Captains Day Cabin, Wind Dancer

┃thank you again for your offer," Will repeated to the tenth
┃person he'd talked to since using the Farley crystal he'd
┃been given by the Mouse. "I regret that my instructions
are to only place it directly into the hands of the Venerable
One himself."

He was in his day cabin, feet propped up on the desk
with the speaker horn of the wave in one hand. In the other
he held his pipe, which he occasionally drew on, blowing
the smoke overhead. Lawrence Rogers sat across from him,
listening while nursing a mug of tea. To look at him, Rogers
thought, you'd have assumed that this was just another ne-
gotiation with a balky customer rather than the play that
made or broke a year's worth of careful work.

"Impossible," answered the tinny voice from the speaker
grill. "The Venerable One does not give audience to white
foreign devils." Will rolled his eyes silently at Rogers.

"Well, I may be foreign," he shot back, "and I may be an
airdevil, but I'm hardly white." He took a draw from his pipe
and then spoke more reasonably. "Now look, I have what
he needs. I'm willing to do any kind of meet up he wants
within reason. Why don't we just do it and everyone gets

happy?" There was a long pause, then what sounded like another voice hissed through the grill.

"Are you the Redman captain they call Hunting Owl, running the ship called Wind Dancer?" it asked.

Both of them winced at the voices' directness. While popular theory held that no one should be able to listen in on a Farley wave call with its matched crystal set, they'd both seen what someone like their own Michael McGuire could do to that theory. 'Tapdancers', as Aetherwave gimickers were known, could listen in on any conversation with the right effort. Even a supposedly private one over a Farley crystal like this was supposed to be. It was for that reason that shady dealings were always understood to be done in nicknames and round about words. Whoever was on the Aetherwave now was either being stupid or insulting, or maybe they were drawing them into a trap.

"Who is this?" Will grated back, feet hitting the floor as he sat upright.

"You will answer the question, or this talk is finished," replied the voice. Rogers caught Wills eye in warning, and shook his head no. Taking a deep breath, Will spoke into the horn.

"Yes, my name if Hunting Owl," Will replied. "And yes to the rest too." Rogers soundlessly threw up his hands in dismay as Will continued.

"Whom am I speaking with, and how do I get to speak with An Fong?" A longer silence this time, then the same voice answered.

"I am merely An Fong's humble servant," the voice said. "You will be met at the tower, and be taken to where you may meet with him. Please have your delivery ready to go upon docking. This talk is now ended."

"Now wait a minute," Will said back. "There are a few more things to settle first!" Another long pause, then the voice replied.

"What 'things' are those?" the voice asked. Will leaned back again, smiling over at Rogers,

"Nothing that shouldn't take more than a moment or two to settle," Will said genially. "Now about the number of people I am bringing to this meet."

Five minutes later, Will disconnected the wave. "There, that was pretty easy in the end don't you think?" He lit his pipe again, billowing clouds into the room. Rogers merely looked at him skeptically.

"So who else will you take with you?" Rogers asked. Will waved out the Lucifer stick he had used to fire his pipe while thinking about it.

"I want you here to come get us if it's needed," he said finally. "Saira and a couple of her best, I'm thinking. Especially someone who speaks Cantonese, as I never learned it. My Mandarin is good enough I think, but I'd rather have my own translator."

"I do not suppose that you would listen to me if I said again this was foolish," Rogers said directly.

"It will be fine, Lawrence," Will said seeking to be reassuring. He then raised an eyebrow at his First Officer in inquiry. "Besides, we already talked about this. This is our chance to really get the dirt on the airships. We have to do this!" Rogers folded his arms across his chest at this, then continued remorselessly.

"Meeting alone with the leader of the largest crime family in Asia without Dancer over your head is not 'fine'," he pointed out. "When I agreed with this, that was the plan. Now you are going to let them take you where-ever-the-hell to meet this leader. A leader, I might add, whose reputation for ruthlessness towards foreigners, especially foreigners who double cross him, is legendary even among our blood-thirsty acquaintances. This is most certainly not 'fine'."

"We are not double crossing him," Will shot back. "We're simply using the delivery to open an exchange of information with him. Besides, Lawrence, we've been over this. If anyone has knowledge of the black raiders' movements in Asia, it will be someone at An Fong's level. We need to do this."

"Do we?" Rogers asked earnestly. "We've done a lot of foolish things over the last five years Will, but this may well be the most foolish yet. We have developed a quite good network of our own, I might point out. Give it more time son; we will catch up to them." Will shook his head and smiled ruefully at this.

"That's just it old man, we're still playing catch up," Will said softly. Somehow his father's gold watch had made its way into his hands. He stroked its cover absently while he spoke.

"They are too big, too dispersed," he said. "Hell, it took us a year just to find out there had to be more than one black airship. Every time we get a lead, the witness winds up dead, or we are too late to catch the ships. I'm tired of chasing them Lawrence; we need to try a different angle."

The 'Black Airship' was a legend found in every airdevil saloon and smoke den from London to Bombay. According to the legend, a huge ghostly black airship could appear from nowhere, causing any airship unlucky enough to cross its path to vanish with it, never to be seen again. Plenty of airships went missing in a given year, mostly unremarked. The world was wide, and air travel was not safe, simply cheaper and faster than anything else. Besides raiders, there were storms, equipment failures, any number of things that could go wrong.

Most thought the Black Airship was a superstition like the infamous Flying Dutchman of the seas, the product of too much gin and hemp. William Hunting Owl and Lawrence Rogers both knew the Black Airships were all too real. They had, in fact, come together five years ago to hunt them down. Will had lost his father to a black airship and Rogers had been cashiered from the BAN after an encounter with one left him with a wrecked airship and a dead crew. They had created Wind Dancer solely to hunt the sky-reavers down with. It had been a wide and winding hunt that not even the ship's crew knew about.

"It is an insane risk Will," the older man said quietly. "What if it turns out that An Fong is their fence and supplier?"

"I had thought of that", Will said with a grin. "That's why I need you with Dancer to come fetch us quick like if things crash on us," he tapped his bracer with a finger. "We can keep in touch with this. I am counting on you to lead a rescue if we need one." Rogers snorted.

"So the new plan is to rely on a bauble for you to call me on at need. I will then weave Wind Dancer through the streets of Hong Kong with the local constabulary and half the British Army following in our wake. Bloody brilliant!" He sighed, casting his eyes towards the wooden ceiling. "At least we won't have to add kidnapping a member of the peerage to our crimes."

"Speaking of which, where is our lady scholar," Will asked, in an attempt to change the conversation. Both Rogers and he knew they were going to go through with the meeting. Lawrence's objections were part of the little dance they did, but both knew that they really had come too far to turn back now. These were the very circumstances that they had manufactured Wind Dancer's reputation as not-outlaw, yet not-law abiding either, sort of grey as it were.

"Last I saw, Arms-Master Brighton and Lady Hadley were just coming in from target practice off the crow's nest. They were giggling like a pair of schoolgirls," Rogers said disapprovingly. Will nodded in satisfaction upon hearing this.

"Good," he said. "That means that Saira must have convinced her to strap up."

"That is another matter I wish to discuss with you," Rogers said his tone one of mild rebuke. "See here Will," he began. "Giving arms to a Lady of the Realm and a British Scholar of all things? Do you really think that she has anything to do with the underworld? " Will blew smoke out of his mouth and set the pipe down on it's holder on his desk. He folded his hands and looked at Rogers.

"I honestly don't know Lawrence," he said seriously. "If Mouse says that her father is poking around smugglers you can be sure it's true. As for Abigail," Rogers noted, but didn't remark on Wills' use of the familiar name. "Well, she's keeping something a secret. Wouldn't be the first time someone was drawn into a mess by their parents. Devi likes her, so does Saira come to that." He stretched and stood up, "she's done us a good turn, so I don't see as it hurts us to spare her a sparkie at least. Like you though, I'll be glad to see her gone."

"Of course," Rogers replied blandly. "While we are talking about women, we really should bring Saira in on the hunt you know. It is about time, I think." Will frowned at him.

"I thought that you didn't approve of Saira, Larry," he remarked.

"Oh I quite don't," Rogers said dryly. "She's willful, disrespectful, shameless, and a host of other things. She is also very, very, deadly, and manages somehow, to keep ship disciple despite both her attitude, and her actions."

"Larry..." Will began. Rogers held up his hand to forestall his next words.

"Consider it for a moment, William," Rogers urged. "Do you really think that she, or any of the crew for that matter, is safer because they are in the dark about what you and I are really hunting? Will we ask them to go up against a Black Airship without them knowing? I have not noticed you doing anything of the sort on any mission we've been on with this crew in the last five years."

"I don't know as you can say that the two cases are the same," Will replied stiffly. "We both agreed that the fewer that knew, the safer it would be for them. That's why only we and Mouse are fully in. We know what can happen to people who ask the wrong questions about Them. They wind up dead." Will said seriously. He crossed his arms, letting his pipe go out.

"When we started this," he continued, "We thought we were only dealing with one airship. As we dug, we found out that there had to be more than one, and that someone, most likely, is running a smart, well connected operation around the world. And what was the price for every piece of knowledge that I just listed? Someone died, Lawrence," he said seriously. "What if someone gets drunk on liberty and lets out that they're hunting Them? Will they make it back to the ship alive?" Will shook his head. "I think that we made a smart call to keep it secret."

"Perhaps so," Rogers said. "However, I'm beginning to think it's time we looked at that decision again. We really didn't think it through, William. I wasn't simply being rhetorical about Dancer facing a Black Airship, it could happen. God help us if we do, as we'll be so outclassed we'll be lucky to soil our breaches before we're dead. But we should consider the possibility."

"I know we've always thought in terms of finding some proof that we could take before the BAN, or if necessary the Allied Expeditionary Force, not that either of us think much of the AEF anymore." Rogers looked at Will tiredly. "Frankly, I am not sure now what proof we could find to convince either organization that we weren't simply barking."

"So what are you saying Lawrence," Will asked softly, "That we should just give up?"

"No, far from it," the First Officer said, crossing his own arms. "To be perfectly frank, I too, am getting tired of 'catch up' as you put it. I am proposing that we look at this as we would a military problem, not a police problem. We have created a fine military instrument here, with the Wind Dancer.

I believe we can trust Brighton. For that matter I believe we can trust the rest of the crew at this point. I doubt that we have any enemy agents among them; some honestly will not care who they fight so long as there's money to be made. A wise general doesn't leave his troops in the dark about the real mission, does he?"

"Maybe so," Will allowed. He looked at Rogers searchingly. "Where is this sudden change coming from Lawrence?"

"I have a feeling," Rogers said, quoting one of Wills favorite responses. Will raised an eyebrow at that.

"Really?" Will asked. Whenever he said that, it meant that Will had received a message from the Spirit Realms. So far as he knew, Rogers was simply a cynical blind man about such things.

"Well, why shouldn't I?" Rogers said testily. "You and that knife wielding witch do so all the time."

"Yes," Will said solemnly, though his eyes sparkled, "But, well, you are English, Lawrence." There came a discreet knock at the door. Will sang out for the knocker to enter and Arms-Master Brighton looked around the door.

"Oh," she said, "I shall return when you are not busy Cap'n," she said, beginning to leave.

"No, wait," Will said to her easily. "Come on in if you have a minute, you'll save me calling a staff meeting. I was just going over with Rogers our strategy for dealing with An Fong when we make landfall." The Hindu warrior nodded, entering the cabin and closing the door behind her.

"Yes," she inquired simply, "and what strange circumstances are we dropping into this time?" She commanded one of the wicker chairs and composed herself to listen. Will told her of his conversation with the voice over the Aetherwave and what his thinking was, Rogers interrupting only occasionally. Saira nodded solemnly when they had finished.

"I would recommend Tikku to accompany us," Saira said without hesitation. "She knows Cantonese as well as Mandarin. She is also very good with the shotgun should we be needing that. I will think on who else." She paused then held up her own bracer.

"If we have two of these present, than it is much more likely that one of them will work," she pointed out. "Still I am with Rogers on this, and would have every member of the landing party carry flares as well in case we need them." Both Will and Lawrence nodded agreement at this.

"What were you coming to see me about?" Will asked her. Saira leaned forward in her chair, eyes moving from one of them to the other.

"I am glad to be talking to you both," she began. "I am just leaving Lady Hadley from target practice with a sparkie." Rogers frowned at this, but said nothing.

"How is she doing?" Will asked curiously. Saira shrugged.

"She is not bad," the Arms-Master opined. "I am surprised at her abilities given that she is a silver-spooned mudfoot. In fact I feel that we should offer her a place on the staff of the ship." Rogers startled at this.

"What?" he exclaimed. "No! Out of the question!" The Arms-Master turned towards him.

"And why would that be?" she demanded. "The Lady Abigail can shoot, she is quite educated and Devi thinks she is a great asset to the Engine Room. Besides," she finished with a glance at the Captain, "I have a feeling." Rogers raised his hands to the heavens in mocking supplication.

"God help us," he said. "Now the Arms-Master has a feeling too!" He turned back towards Will. "You surely cannot take this idea seriously."

"Why not?" Saira asked archly. "It would not be because she is one of your lily-white ladies would it?" Rogers sputtered at this.

"No!" he said heatedly. "Besides the facts that she is both a Scholar and a peer of the realm, she is a mudfoot!" He turned towards Will. "We do not have the time to train someone so green." Will had turned his face down towards his chin listening to them both. Now he turned his face up towards Saira.

"What makes you think that she would accept an offer where we to make one?" He asked her calmly. Saira shrugged.

"My feeling is all," she said calmly. "I know that she will be important to this ship in some manner I have yet to see. I urge us to take her on board." Will nodded.

"She is used to living a very different kind of life, you know," he said to her. "How about this, I will think on the idea, and see if I think she would welcome it. You don't say anything to her one way or the other. The only way I would take her on is if she really wants on."

"That seems only sensible," Rogers said agreeably. "I just wish that there was some other way I could follow where you are going from Dancer." Saira shrugged.

"If wishes where fish, we would all cast nets," she said philosophically. "Know that we shall keep the Cap'n safe and succeed in the mission." She frowned at them both. "This is all that there is to the mission yes? There is not more that I need to know?" Rogers spared a glance towards his Captain.

"I believe that it is past time that I relieved the deck," he began to rise from his chair. Will held out a hand.

"No Larry," Will said to him, "I think that you should stay right here. It is only fitting' to my mind." He turned in his chair to look at the Arms-Master.

"Saira, there is more to this mission than a simple drop off. It is the information we hope to get from An Fong."

Saira nodded enthusiastically on hearing this.

"Good," she said approvingly. "It is about time that you shared what your secret mission is." She laughed at the look of amazement on both of the men's faces.

The laughter turned solemn as she listened to Will's story of receiving that last Aetherwave message from his father as their merchant airship, and Will's home, was destroyed by the Black Airships. She listened while Rogers described his encounter while in command of HMS Defiant, describing the enemy airship with an emotionless tone that spoke more loudly than screams every could. She sighed into the silence that followed.

"So," she said finally. "If I am understanding this, we are hunting a legend which is not a legend at all but shadowy real." The two men nodded. "We have no idea who they are, or where they may be, but we are thinking that they must sell their booty as other pirates do, so we are taking a valuable possession of a Chinese underground leader back to him in hopes that he will tell us more about these shadowy figures in exchange for it."

"That about sums it up," Will said dryly. "So, now that you know, are you still in?"

She looked at him almost angrily.

"Why should that even be a question?" she asked. "Of course I am 'in'. I have given you oath to the Articles, yes?" She shrugged. "If we are hunting demons then it is easy. When we find them we kill them."

"It is not quite that easy," Rogers objected. "We have been hunting them for five years now. Nor do I think that they are some sort of supernatural beings, merely murderous and invisible to authority." Saira nodded.

"As I said," she pronounced with satisfaction, "Demons." She looked at them both, "This is in keeping with my visions. Is there anything else I need to be doing?" Will shook his head.

"No Saira, I do not think so." He pulled on a braid, regarding her thoughtfully. "I must say though, that you are taking this all a mite easier than I thought you would." She shrugged again.

"I was thinking that your secret purpose must be something truly unpleasant," she said. "To find that it is merely hunting mysterious enemies across the world is so much better than what I thought." Will started to open his mouth at this, then thought better of it and closed it.

"Well, I am glad to have you in on everything at last," he said instead. Saira smiled at him

"And glad I am to be included in everything." She replied brightly. "Although there is much more that I wish to know, I will wait for the moment as we are coming up on watch change." She looked at Mr. Rogers pointedly. "Is it not?" Rogers stirred himself up out of his chair.

"Indeed," he grumbled, "I had best go see to turnover." Hunting Owl waved him back.

"A minute of your time there, Larry," he requested. "I'll see to the watch change." Although neither Rogers nor Will were on the bridge watch list, as they were always on call, it was customary for one of them to be present at the Bridge turn-over. Saira raised her hand, as she was already near the door.

"I will oversee the turn-over," she volunteered. "It is clear that you have more to discuss." Will nodded at her.

"Thank you, Arms-Master," he said formally. "Inform the officer of the watch that I will be there shortly." Saira turned and ghosted out the door, closing it firmly behind her. Will looked at Rogers.

"Well," he said easily to his First Officer, "that pretty well don't you think?" Rogers nodded briskly.

"Not exactly the time and place I would have chosen," Rogers said, "but it worked. You are about to go into the proverbial lion's den this time Will, and someone else on the ground who knows what we are up against, and what we are trying to accomplish could mean all the difference." Rogers continued, "The Dancer won't be right there to back you up, and I am truly concerned." He looked down at the watch still in Will's hand and then back up to his eyes. "Getting killed won't bring him back you know," he said softly.

"No, it won't," Will replied just as softly. "But there is something bigger going on here, something awful and mean. You know as well as I that there's more here than a bunch of renegades out to pirate. They're too big for just that." Will looked down at the watch, caressing it, and then at Rogers soberly.

"My real fear is that a whole bunch of kids will wake up without a father someday soon if we do not stop them. So we are going ahead with this. Besides," Rogers noticed that the watch had vanished into Hunting Owls vest. "I promised his ghost I'd see them all dead," he said simply. "I'll be on the bridge if you need me." Will walked out, closing his cabin door behind him.

"We all have ghosts, son," Rogers replied sadly to the closed door.

# Chapter Fifteen

*Wind Dancer*, Hong Kong Harbor

The next morning, Abigail donned her travel dress for the first time since boarding Wind Dancer. While it had been repaired and cleaned, she had not felt the need to wear it while on board. Her tunic, vest and pants had seemed quite the right thing. Now though, as she was re-entering the formal world, it was time to wear the proper dress for the occasion. It took some time to lace her corset; a task that was normally difficult enough to do on one's own, was made even more difficult by the after effects of the previous evening's soirée.

While it hadn't seemed planned to her, most of those whom she had come to know had appeared in the mess to wish her well.

There had been Devi, Saira and the Captain of course, but she was surprised how many others had come as well. She frowned, trying to remember the evening, an effort that made her head hurt. She recalled tiny cakes presented by Doctor Wu, with little thimble-size glasses of a clear liquor. Many glasses, she recalled. There had been songs, and jokes, then more little glasses. She hazily recalled that she had been warned that the little glasses had contained a much more potent liquor than the usual ration, a Chinese brew that Doctor Wu had introduced whenever there was a leave–taking on the ship, or she had been told. It must be the after-effects of that she was feeling.

As she finished struggling into her short dove grey traveling jacket, she frowned. It wasn't as if she was likely to see any of them ever again, she realized. She found that the thought made her suddenly very sad. She had never really felt as if she belonged in any group of people before. She almost wished...but such thoughts were absurd; besides she was soon to see her father, and wrestle with a greater destiny. A knock at the door interrupted her thoughts. Saira breezed in, a mug of tea in one hand, an electric pistol in the other.

"Ah, good morning! I see you are already dressed," she said. "Good. Here," she held out the mug. "Did you put on the holster as I showed you?"

Abigail gratefully took the mug from her hand as the Arms-Master knelt in front of her. She drank deeply from the mug before replying, savoring the strong ship tea filled with spices and milk.

"Yes," Abigail replied, "although I still don't see why I can't simply—hey there!" She yelped as Saira lifted her skirts and underskirts, checking the fit of the holster against her thigh. Abigail decided to stop moving, and drank more of the tea. "As I said yesterday, if you carry it in a bag, it will take you too long to reach when you need it," Saira said patiently. "This is not buckled tight enough. Hold still." She pulled straps tighter for a few moments while Abigail struggled not to move.

"There," Saira set back on her heels. "Now move your leg." Abigail did so, finding to her surprise that it actually felt better. When she said so, Saira nodded.

"Always pull it that tight, believe me that you do not want it chafing." She explained to the Scholar while standing up. She held out the pistol to Abigail.

"Here is your weapon, a Webley Thunderbolt," Saira continued in the dry voice of a professional. She pointed as she spoke. "It is fully charged, meter here. Switch set to off, here. You check it," she ordered, handing it butt first to Abigail.

Abigail took the pistol, setting down her mug. It had a short 'barrel' with two smaller barrels projecting from it. These housed the invisible light projectors on which the current was guided to its target. The pistol felt heavier than it looked, as most of the weapon was simply a large battery. She checked the lenses and dials herself under Saira's watchful eye.

"Right then," Abigail said finally. She moved to place it in the holster on her leg. Saira had arranged for slits in her skirts that were cleverly concealed by hooks which closed along the outer fold. Abigail slid the gun through the slit, and then drew it as quickly as she could. While the pistol did not catch on anything Abigail felt clumsy doing so. Saira shook her head at the attempt.

"Try again," Saira ordered, in her professional role as Arms-Master.

This time it felt faster and smoother. Abigail flushed as she placed it back in its holster, and smiled at the other woman. She felt as if she was some heroine in a serial. Saira returned the smile.

"Better," the Arms-Master said. "You will improve as you practice. Although you must not think that carrying a weapon makes you invincible," she warned. "What does help you is if you realize that when you decide to draw it, it must be to defend your life or the life of another. Then there must be no thinking, no hesitation. Draw and fire that is all. Think on this and try again."

Abigail nodded at her words, which sobered her considerably. She settled down, and then imagined her father in danger. She drew swiftly, thumb already on the selector switch before she was aware that she had done so. Saira nodded approvingly.

"Much better," the Arms-Master said. Will poked his head through the door and grinned.

"That's what I like to see," he said, "a Scholar who's armed as well as smart! I stopped down because I thought you might like to see us dock." Abigail ruefully returned the gun to its holster. She had learned that airdevils had a different sensibility when it came to privacy.

"I am not convinced that going armed to the necessity is particularly 'smart'," she greeted the Captain wryly. "But I bow to the knowledge of the experts in the field." She gave a small curtsy, which both of the others returned with a bow. She laughed in surprise.

"Come now!" she objected. "Please do not go all proper on me at this junction! And yes, Captain, I would love to see docking if I may."

Abigail noticed that Will was wearing a long dress coat instead of his usual vest and gun belt. He still wore his goggles around his neck, and the large knife called a 'Bowie' was still visible at his waist. It was then that Abigail noticed that Saira also wore a long coat as well. Her pants covered legs brazenly sticking out of the long folds.

"You both seem to be rather formally dressed today," Abigail remarked. Will pulled a breathing mask out of a pocket.

"Disembarking togs," Will said shortly. "Rogers thought that you might find this an easier way to breathe in that muck they call air outside," he said, handing the breather towards her. She held the face covering device awkwardly in one hand.

"Thank you," Abigail said distantly. "If it is all the same to you, I shall wait until I need it, before putting it on." Saira nodded at her.

"They can be uncomfortable," Saira said easily. "They only stopped wearing them in Calcutta with the armistice, when they kept the Shield down. Shall we go to the docking then Milady?" She asked Abigail with a drawl and an exaggerated sniff. Will held out his own arm as well. Still laughing Abigail placed a hand on both arms.

"By all means then, my gallants," she cried. "Do lead on!"

"Very good, Milady, Will drawled with a sniff of his own. "This way if you please, do watch out for the grouse, don't you know?" Laughing the three of them swept down the corridors.

Upon reaching the bridge, Abigail looked around in fascination. She had not been here since the meeting in the Captain's day cabin. At the time, she had not felt she could indulge her curiosity. It was as large as the engine room, easily some thirty feet across. She saw the stations at which sat various people she knew. Occasionally one of them would silently wave at her, and then turn back to their boards. Mr. Rogers stood at the front, looking through an electric lens. Then, she looked beyond him out the large windows, and gave a soft gasp.

The view before her was of a toy city nestled in a harbor, encased in a shining soap bubble that was shimmering all the colors of the rainbow. She knew that the shimmer was the city's Shield, but she had never seen one from this perspective before. The ring of what looked like tiny mushrooms that surrounded the city were the Shield towers. Around the bubble, like minnows, swam airships either coming or going. What looked like a small school of ships floated before the bubble as if waiting to be let inside the shield. Rogers turned at her gasp and briefly smiled at her, then turned towards Will.

"Captain, Lady Hadley," he acknowledged. "We have just received word that the shield will open in about ten minutes." Will let go of Abigail's arm and strode down the short ramp, then between the stations to stand beside his First Officer.

"I have the bridge, Lawrence," he said bending to look through the lens that Rogers had just been looking through.

"Aye, Aye, the Captain has the bridge," Rogers acknowledged formally. He pointed out towards the city, speaking to Hunting Owl in a quieter voice.

Saira poked Abigail in the arm, miming walking with her fingers. She next pointed to where the Captain had moved, and then held a finger against her lips. Abigail startled, then quietly nodded, and they made their way across the floor to stand behind the two men.

"Looks good to me," Will said. Without turning he called out to the wave station, "Michael," he called out, "what does Hong Kong Port Authority say?"

"HKPA has just given us instructions for approach," the wave operation reported headphone held against one ear. "They say everything is fine. I'm not picking up any trouble from the public Aetherwave or from any connection I can reach." He frowned, turning a dial. "There is a lot of fuzz though, and some connections that I should be getting, I'm not."

"What are the instructions, Mr. McGuire?" Rogers asked. McGuire read them off a paper at his station. Rogers and Will exchanged a glance.

"Sounds normal to me," Will said. "Let's take her in, Lawrence."

"Aye Aye Captain," Rogers began issuing a series of commands.

Abigail looked back out on the city, seeing that they had now arrived much closer to the 'school' of airships she had noticed earlier. They all seemed to be floating in stillness before the rainbow sheen.

"If I may ask," she said, "do you know why the city has its Shield raised? Most cities that I am familiar with only raise them for drills." The Tesla Shield was one of the great inventions of the War. A city-sized force field that rendered it virtually impenetrable to attack. Shields had almost returned humanity to a series of feudal states, where it huddled inside the shield wall.

"Well," Will explained, "here in China beyond that Shield what you mostly find is penny-packet warlords that all pretty much hate it that the British still hold one of the only two real cities left in the country. The Chinese hold a grudge something powerful. As some of those warlords have airships of their own, the Shield stays up." Will continued, I'm told that things are so bad in the countryside that people work real hard to be able to live under the protection of it."

"How horrible," Abigail said. "But surely they must drop it sometimes; else the air would become extremely unhealthy with that many people inside."

Rogers came back to stand with them.

"I have been here before, Milady," he said. "The air is so foul in the city, coal smoke, cooking fires, not to mention the number of people that breathing masks are common among the citizens. While they do open it for traffic a few times daily, it is on an irregular schedule, and never for long enough to clear the air, so to speak. We are fortunate that we have arrived close to one of those times. Of course, they could be telling us the wrong time," he smiled without humor. He glanced at his pocket watch again and turned to Will, "Shield opening is in seven minutes, Captain. We are holding station until then."

"Very good, Lawrence," Will acknowledged. "Please advance us to berth when it opens."

"Aye Aye, Captain," Rogers replied. He walked over to Naomi Walker, the bridge talker, leaving the three of them standing before the sight of the huge rainbow in front of them.

"I've always found Shields to be very beautiful," Saira remarked.

"It is a pretty sight that is for a fact," Will agreed. "I've always wanted to ask someone who might know," he said, looking at Abigail, "What makes it so colorful?" Abigail opened her mouth to answer, than closed it again with a frown that Will recognized as the same kind of frown that Devi wore when asked about the engines.

"How much do you know about Shields?" Abigail asked. It was Will's turn to frown.

"Well," he said scratching his chin, "I know that anything solid that touches one gets ripped apart, whether it be a ship, a rocket, or a person. I know that things like the Invaders heat rays and smoke can't get through them either. That they take really big Tesla engines to power, which is why we can't make smaller ones. Oh," he said snapping his fingers, "and that stuff like coal smoke and the like can't get through it either, but that air can."

"Right," Abigail sighed. "Well, you know that a Tesla engine takes the energy of the earth and transfers it into a form that we can channel into electricity? We call it the Tellurian Effect." Both Will and Saira nodded. "What a Shield tower does is take that same energy and runs it from one tower to its opposite in the ring. The way the energy is run causes the towers to create a 'dome' of highly energized air which illuminates in the colors of the spectrum."

"Like the gas in light tubes," Will said. Abigail smiled,

"Exactly. Only instead of being certain gases that create light in one color, this is exciting the air itself."

"And this energy is like electricity which is why it stops everything," Saira nodded. A look like pain crossed Abigail's features

"Not exactly," she said. "The 'rainbow' is the air itself becoming energized. There is simply so much air that some interpenetrates." She paused, "Do either of you have any understanding of Aetheric theory?"

"Only that Aether is everywhere but we can't touch it," Will said blandly.

"Oh," Abigail paused for a moment then spoke, "Well, the Aether is actually another dimension. This dimension is the bedrock if you will, of the universe that we can touch and see all around us. The Shield effect is just strong enough to create a 'place' in the Aether itself, unlike the Aetherwave, which 'tunnels' through the Aether, connecting two places in this universe instantly," She stopped, seeing their pained expressions as they tried to follow her.

"Yes, it's something like electricity," she finally allowed in mild despair. "Only we can make it hard as a stone wall." Will and Saira both nodded their understanding at this.

"Thirty seconds to opening," Rogers announced. "Mark."

"Have you ever seen this Abigail?" Will whispered. "Watch," he pointed forward.

When Rogers count reached 'one', suddenly the shimmer vanished in a slice directly in front of them. Behind the open section they could see a haze that melted into a stream of grey smoke that flowed towards the ground, moving out from the city. The ships in front of them began moving forward, and at Rogers command the Wind Dancer moved as well, passing beyond the wall of shimmering color to either side of them.

"Mr. Jarro," Rogers said, "Our tower is blue south, berth number ten."

"Blue tower two points to port, berth ten one hundred feet elevation" called out one of the lookouts at the lenses.

The tattooed Maori at the helm and the Japanese woman at the elevator wheel both repeated these words back, turning the ship smoothly. Abigail watched as they approached a round tower with blue lights atop it and down its sides. She watched as the tower grew larger in front of them. They glided towards a slip that had a yards high number ten painted on it, above and below the slip were other airships already docked.

"All stop." Rogers called. Abigail heard Naomi relay the order. The constant hum that Abigail had become so used to suddenly stopped. The ship continued to drift forward in the silence until Rogers called out, "Fire grapples!" Abigail saw harpoon lines snake out to strike colored places on the wall of the tower. "Reel forward," Rogers called. She saw the lines go taut as the ship winches slowly pulled the large ship closer to the tower. She saw the slip rush up towards them from below. There was a slight bump, and then Rogers called out, "All stop. Secure to berth."

"That was a smooth berthing," Will whispered in Abigail's ear. "They're the best air devils in the sky you know." There was no mistaking the pride in his voice.

"Chief Marsh reports riggers have secured to berth," Naomi called out.

"Thank you Mr. Walters," Rogers said. He turned towards Will. "Captain, ship is secured to berth. Recommend that stations lock and Tesla Engines go to idle."

"Make it so Mr. Rogers," Will said formally.

"Mr. Jarro, Mr. Matori, lock and stand down." Abigail watched as Jarro and Matori locked their wheels and stepped away from them.

"Well done everyone," Will said. "Naomi, my compliments to the crew and stand to berth watch stations. No liberty call until announced."

"Aye, Aye, Captain, stand to berth watch stations. No liberty call until announced." The bridge talker spoke into her speaker horn. When she finished, she looked back up. "Please tell me that I can go get some chocolate soon Cap'n." She pleaded. Will smiled at her.

"Soon as our business is done, I'll buy you a big box myself," he promised. The bridge talker's face lit up in a smile of her own. Will turned back to Abigail still smiling. He gave her a courtly bow. "Welcome to Hong Kong, Lady Hadley," he said.

## Chapter Sixteen

Wind Dancer, Air Tower, Hong Kong

Will accompanied Abigail to fetch her lone bag. The Captain promised her that her instrument trunk would be unloaded and sent to the hotel where she said she was to meet her father. Together, they made their way back to the hatch that would be connected to the passenger sky bridge. Each berth had a bridge for passengers and crew that was extended out from tower. The ship floated above the landing strip itself which was used to load and unload cargo. Captain Hunting Owl assured her that Saira and Rogers would meet them there, so that she might say her farewells.

"There's a little dance we have to go through with customs before we can actually set foot off the ship," Will explained.

"What kind of dance?" Abigail asked.

"Oh, nothing much, really," the Captain said with a wave of his hand. "Just arranging for how we're paying for dock space and service, what we're bringing in to port, that kind of thing. Some places it could take us all day just to sort it out and pay the right bribes. Being a British colony, Hong Kong is pretty easy as these things go. We have already declared, and all that, over the wave. I have found that gold bars work pretty well for services and bond surety." He grinned at her with the last statement.

"I see," Abigail mused. "I hadn't really considered that essentially you are as much a business as any merchant or passenger ship. That you have to concern yourself with such things seems positively prosaic after the way we met. "

"What," Will laughed, "did you think that we get free lift gas and supplies just for being glamorous mercenaries?" He stroked the feather at the back of his hair, and then straightened his vest. "Although I do admit we are a stirringly handsome bunch."

"And as modest as your Arms-Master, I see!" Abigail responded with a laugh.

"I reckon that you will be pleased to see your father," Will remarked as they walked. Abigail's face lit up with a smile.

"Oh yes," she enthused, "Seeing Papa will be ever so grand! And the work we have yet to do." She cut herself off and turned towards him. "I am exceedingly grateful for your assistance. I promise you that as soon as possible I shall see to it that you are reimbursed for all your trouble." The Captain waved her offer away.

"You haven't been any trouble, Lady Hadley," Will assured her. "In fact, to listen to my engineer I should pay you for your help." He glanced at her sideways. "You could always make a living selling that skill to an airship you know." Abigail smiled at this.

"Why thank you Captain." She looked ahead, as if seeing into the future. "Should I ever need employment I shall keep what you say in mind. While the thought is tempting, the work my father and I are doing is important!" Hunting Owl nodded at this.

"That's' what I figured," Will said causally.

"But I do appreciate the fact that I need not wear skirts aboard!" She said with a laugh.

"Maybe you could start a new fashion." The Captain said.

"Oh I hardly think so!" Abigail exclaimed. "I cannot see most women preferring pants over skirts."

"Do not the northern men of your island wear skirts as well? Lots of countries where men do," Will pointed out.

"Would you like to wear a skirt yourself, Captain?" Abigail asked him, a light playing in her eyes.

"Nope," Will said definitely. "My knees are way too bony to look any good. Besides," He said patting his revolver. "I could not draw as quickly as you can." Abigail laughed. Will joined her.

They were both still laughing when they turned the corner to find Rogers and Saira waiting before the still closed hatch.

"What seems to be our hold up, Lawrence?" Will asked.

"Still waiting on the customs," Rogers said looking out the door porthole. "Ah, here he comes at last." Rogers pushed open the door by its lock wheel.

Before anyone could speak, in strode a rat-faced florid little man with a pencil mustache and a swagger stick under his arm. He was followed by a taller man with a clipboard in his hands. Two stone-faced Chinese Sepoy's with rifles at port arms stopped just inside the hatch. They were all dressed in the dark blue of the Queens Port Authority. The little man walked up to Mr. Rogers.

"I am Inspector Nilquist of Customs and Immigration," he announced. "I presume you are the captain of this," here he gave a slightly curl of his lip, "vessel?" Will stepped forward, thumbs in his belt, his foot long Bowie knife prominently displayed.

"I'm Captain Hunting Owl, and this is my First Officer, Mr. Rogers," he explained calmly. "How can we help you today, Inspector?" The Inspector looked at Will as if he'd discovered a cockroach in his salad.

"You are the Captain?" Nilquist asked incredulously. Will gave an easy nod.

"Captain and Owner of the Wind Dancer out of Seattle Freeport, licensed for trade and bonded," Will replied. "Oh, we also bear letters of Marque from both the Seattle Council and the East India Company. I believe we already transmitted our authenticity codes, and manifest to Port Control, but my First Officer here has the papers for your inspection, Inspector. Lawrence, if you would please." The man with the clipboard took the thick stack that Mr. Rogers held. Nilquist, whose color had gone a deeper red, sniffed.

"This will all have to be verified of course," the Inspector looked around the airlock with a sour pucker to his lips. Rogers had gone stiff at the man's tone, while Will continued in his half slouch, looking at the inspector through lidded eyes.

"I'm sure that we can come to some understanding here Inspector," Will said easily. "We have cargo that must be unloaded quickly. Would fifty pounds sterling in gold bullion be sufficient for our surety bond?" The inspector's face was a fleeting study in surprise. Fifty pounds would keep a family of four for an entire year. The usual port fees would never amount to more than half that much. Nilquist narrowed his eyes.

"I see," He looked at Will, calculating. "Well, we have added new port fees you may not be aware of. Ninety pounds would cover your fee." Will met the man's gaze directly.

"Well that is a might higher than we were planning on, Inspector," the Captain said. "We do have the fifty right here." Will pointed a thumb at Saira, who held up a small strong box for the Inspector to see.

Abigail decided that it was time she intervened, before things got out of hand altogether. She may not know much, but she did know that ninety pounds was tantamount to robbery. Why she could have traveled all the way here by air for that amount! She would not stand for a repeat of the exploitation that she experienced in Bombay. Stepping out from behind Rogers and Saira, she spoke sharply in her best savant speaking voice.

"This is hardly the behavior I would expect from a Queen's Servant, Inspector," she said in rebuke. The little man, now purple faced, rounded towards her, slicing his stick through the air.

"And I could give a damn what some pox ridden doxy thinks!" His rant cut off, as he caught sight of Abigail in her gray London travel dress with the Scholar's crest on the left breast. Wordlessly she removed a glove and touched the jewel in the crest's center, which began to give a pale blue glow.

He went slack-jawed, his eyes bulging, as he watched the glow. Abigail was suddenly grateful for what she had always considered a showy bit of frippery. The crest of every member of the Order was set with a small galvanic conductor, which would only glow at the touch of the person keyed to it. The means of making of them was a Crown secret. They unmistakably marked the owner as being of the Orders, or of the Queen's Eyes, her Majesty's Secret Service, depending on the color of the gem.

"I am Abigail, Lady Hadley of the Royal Order of Scholars," she announced. "You will address me as Lady Hadley." The man closed his mouth, and practically jumped to attention. "As I said, I find this behavior most unseemly in a Queen's Officer, Mister?" She paused for effect, raising an eyebrow.

"Nilquist, Lady Hadley," he gulped, "Inspector Harold Nilquist."

"Well, Mr. Nilquist, you can be assured that your attitude will be mentioned in my reports. For your information, Captain Hunting Owl and his crew have been of great service to me and hence, to the Order." She said in acerbic tones. Abigail had always hated any sort of officious bullying, which was part of why Bombay had left such a bad taste in her mouth. This time, she could do something about it. This colonial idiot would see what officious bullying could really be like. He swallowed hard, eyes looking around as if for some escape.

"Forgive me Lady Hadley," the Inspector said. "I had no idea this vessel was under your employ."

"Perhaps, if you had spoken with the courtesy of a Queen's Officer at the beginning, you would have ascertained some facts," she replied coldly.

"Yes, Lady Hadley," He said meekly.

"Now, of your courtesy, you will make whatever arrangements are required, for the fastest disembarkation possible from this ship. I have much to do, and I'm sure Captain Hunting Owl has business of his own." She inclined her head towards Will, who with a straight face nodded back.

"Yes, Lady Hadley," Nilquist became ramrod straight, and shot out his left arm. "Smothers!" he barked. The other man quickly handed him the clipboard, and stepped back into his own attention position.

"Declared cargo, purpose of visit, and estimated length?" The Inspector droned out in true bureaucratic form, pencil hovering over the forms.

"Private cargo for Yang Imports, Customs pre-declared and duties paid. Delivery, resupply, and shore leave about one week at the outside. Oh, and one passenger," Will pointed at Abigail with his thumb, and then grinned at the man.

The now stone-faced man wrote hurriedly on many forms, tore off several which he handed to Mr. Rogers, along with the ships papers. "I declare that all seems to be in order. We can take your berth surety to the Port Master's office for you."

Saira wordlessly held up the case. Looking at the cold blue eyes in Saira's dark face, Nilquist hesitated for a moment, before beginning to reach for it. Abigail decided that she simply would not stand for it.

"Inspector," she said innocently, "Forgive me, but I thought that the ship officers would be taking that to the Office themselves? I'm sure that you have other ships to see to, do you not?" Nilquist's arms froze; he lowered them slowly, and then wiped his hands against his trousers.

"Yes, of course, My Lady," he said weakly. Abigail noticed Smothers trying determinedly not to look crestfallen, while she caught the two guard's mouths quirk upwards for the briefest moment. Clearly, they did not receive part of the bribes.

"Of course," Will said smoothly, "we actually have quite a lot to do. I would be most obliged if you would see to that little detail for us, Inspector."

The inspector smiled weakly, "Thank you Captain, you're very kind," he said eyes on Abigail's stern face. His arm swung up again quickly, and took the case from Saira, tucking it protectively under one arm.

"Is there anything else I might do for you My Lady? Captain Hunting Owl?" he asked unctuously.

Will made a show of looking at Rogers, then Abigail, before turning back. He seemed to be enjoying Nilquist's discomfort. He waved a hand lazily.

"Oh we're perfectly fine," he said lazily, "Inspector, perfectly fine. Thank you for your attentions." Nilquist snapped a sharp salute at Will that should have dislocated his shoulder.

"Then welcome to Hong Kong, Captain, and Lady Hadley." He turned, barking orders. "Smothers! You lot!" He said, gesturing at the guards. "Stop standing around! Come on! Move! Move!" He strode briskly out the doorway, past the guards, striding down the bridge.

Saira began to giggle softly as soon as they were out of earshot, Will grinned at Abigail outright. Even Rogers smiled faintly as he gave the Scholar a short bow from the waist.

"Well played, Milady," Rogers murmured, "Well played indeed."

"I do hope that I have not caused a problem for you." Abigail looked at them, brushing away strands of hair from her face. "I do apologize if I have, but even I could see that ninety pounds was unreasonable."

"You do right well, Lady Abigail," Will grinned at her. "He got his fair squeeze as the port fees only amount to about twenty pounds all up. I don't mind the cost of business, but I'd as soon not spend half the day dickering with a port bandit." He nodded at her jacket crest. "I had no idea that was such a useful bauble."

"Yes well," Abigail stroked the crest for a moment, and the blue gem glow faded. She looked up at him startled. "Twenty pounds you say? The man should be reported!"

"Please do not," Saira said seriously. "As Cap'n Will says it is the way of things." She grinned. "You should see what Customs does to you English in Free India." Then she frowned in thought. "If you do peach on him," Saira said," we will gain the reputation of being a 'trouble ship'. It will be harder for us here and elsewhere from then on. Customs people talk almost as much as air devils do."

"Very good then," Rogers said. "Now that the customs have been so thoroughly dealt with," he nodded at Abigail, "I shall go see to our cargo. You will doubtless want to greet the business people yourself Captain," he remarked to Will.

"Thank you Lawrence," Will said. "Let's just run things as we discussed." He tapped his communications bracer discreetly.

"Aye, aye, Captain," Rogers said and turned back to Abigail, bowing again. "Lady Hadley, it has been a distinct pleasure to make your acquaintance. Your presence aboard has been a true joy. May I say again, good show on dealing with Nilquist.  Good luck, and good fortune."

"Thank you Mr. Rogers, Abigail inclined her head regally. "The pleasure has been all mine, I assure you. As for that popinjay," she twisted her shoulders, "I despise bullying, especially officious bullying."

"Quite so," Rogers agreed. He braced to and saluted her, "Safe journey to you, my Lady." He walked back up ship leaving the three of them standing in the lock.

"I am not well practiced at saying thank you," Abigail looked at Will and Saira. She squared her shoulders. "Thank you. It has been an honor to meet you all," the Scholar said. Saira gave Will a look and held out her arms towards Abigail.

"It is we who are honored by meeting you, Lady Abigail." She reached forward and the two women embraced.

"This is not good-bye, my sister," Saira whispered gently in her ear. "Why, is this one of your visions?" Abigail whispered back. "Yes," Saira replied simply. Pulling their heads back, the two locked gazes, then parted.

Abigail turned towards the captain. She was finding all this leave-taking surprisingly difficult. She almost wished, then banished the thought before she could finish it. She had duties to attend to that allowed no room for wishes. She straightened again. "Captain Hunting Owl" she said, "I am eternally in your debt."

"Likewise," Will said. "Hope all goes well with your father. You do have our wave connection, right?" Abigail nodded.

"Yes. Saira also gave me a Farley crystal, thank you. I have also given the Aetherwave address of the hotel to Saira."

Will nodded, "Call us if you want anything, alright? I'd like to meet your father too while we're in port," he paused as if he would say more, then shrugged his shoulders. "Walk in beauty, Lady Hadley."

"I am sure he would like to meet you as well" she replied with a smile. "Godspeed Captain Hunting Owl." She set her shoulders, hefting her bag. "Right then," she said to no one is particular. She turned, and with determination walked down the sky bridge towards the tower. Will and Saira watched her silently until she vanished inside.

"You are an idiot you know, I have seen that the ship will need her." Saira said to him at last.

"That is 'you are an idiot, Captain,'" Will corrected mildly. "Everyone has to follow their own path Saira, even against one of your visions."

"We will see her again you know," Saira continued with a certainty.

"Maybe," Will allowed. "But that is not for us to worry about now." He stirred from his slouch near the hatch, turning towards her. "Come on, let us go make a delivery to a shadowy underworld figure." He looked at Saira sideways, as they walked down the corridors to the loading bay. "You briefed the rest of the party?" She nodded as they walked.

"I have chosen Georgios to accompany us," she said. "He is good with the close fighting, and is level-headed. I would like to bring all the Tigers, but your limit will not let me."

"It's not my limit," Will reminded her. "It's the limit placed by An Fong's people. It wouldn't be much of a friendly sit-down if we brought a bunch of rubber armored airdevils." Saira sniffed at this.

"I fail to see why not," she returned archly. "It is not as if you are not bringing him what he prizes for free."

"That is as may be," Will allowed. "But I do hope to charge him for it."

Well," Saira said as they entered the loading bay, "Both Tikku and Georgios are ready. As is the way of things here in Hong Kong neither is opening carrying a firearm although Georgios is carrying that hatchet of his, and Tikku her fighting sticks, on their belts. Both do have repeating shotguns in discreet cases" She padded her knife hilts.

"I, of course," she added, "have these as well as a hidden sparkie pistol. You?"

"Good choices", Will approved. He slid back his coat so that Saira could see the shoulder holster that held his revolver. He nodded greetings to Tikku and Georgios who were standing in the landing bay awaiting them along with

First Officer Rogers who held the box they had recovered from the slaver's ship.

"Anyone have any questions before we head out?" Will asked looking around at the room. When no one responded, he nodded in satisfied, then turned towards Saira, holding up his bracer.

"Let's check that these work shall we?" he said, pushing the appropriate button. Saira followed suit. Will spoke into the air above his wrist.

"Wind Dancer, Wind Dancer," Will chanted. "This is Hunting Owl, do you receive me?" McGuire's voice answered from the bracer.

"I hear you fine, Cap'n," The voice said. "Is Brighton standing near you with her bracer on?" Saira nodded, then realizing that the Aetherwave officer could not see her, spoke to her wrist.

"Yes, I am," she said.

"I did tell you that you shouldna be doing that," he answered his brogue thickening as he spoke. "I can adjust for the interference, but only just." Captain Hunting Owl looked at his Arms-Master who waved her arms in annoyance at this.

"Sorry about that Michael," Will responded. "We will try to not stand so close together. I want to leave this connection open as we discussed."

"Fine from this end Cap'n," McGuire responded. "Wind Dancer standing by."

Will turned towards Rogers, holding out his hands for An Fong's box.

"Well," he said to his First Officer, "Looks like we are on." Rogers handed him the box, shaking his head doubtfully.

"I still am not convinced on the wisdom of relying on this ground to air talking," Rogers said to him in a low voice. "But message us and we will come running." The officer promised.

Will grinned at him.

"Let's hope that there is no need for that Larry," he answered. "Remember you are to do nothing unless you hear me say so."

Rogers nodded at this. "Understood," he replied shortly. After an awkward pause he said, "Good hunting." Will nodded silently at him, choosing to leave much unspoken. He then turned towards Saira and her Tigers.

"Let's be about this then," he said, leading the way down the loading ramp.

~~~

Hu was dressed as any other rising young zhu shou who worked in one of the near-by office buildings would be. He was wearing a brown Western-style suit and tie with slicked back short hair. As such he was completely unremarkable from the dozens of others like him. Given that he made his living by being anonymous, anyone would be forgiven for not catching on that he was following them. A fact which would have been of small comfort to Saira and her Tigers, had they known at the time.

However, she and the others were busy looking for more obvious threats, so the busy young modern man in the crowded modern air tower went completely unremarked.

Hu witnessed the meeting of the Wind Dancer crew with An Fong's representatives in the basement garage of the Air Tower where the steamcars were parked.

After what appeared to be many introductions, the group drove up the exit ramp in one of the more luxurious steam cars. Hu hefted the box that he carried on a shoulder strap while looking about the garage. Finding a secluded spot, he opened the box, pulling out a speaking horn and earmuff. As he cranked the handle to power it up he knew a moments pride at having been entrusted with one of the far-speaking devices the White Lady of Death herself had distributed among the gangs. He held the ear piece and spoke into the horn as he had been taught.

"This is Hu," he reported. "The package is being taken to An Fong by the Redman Captain. There are four of them, and four of An Fong's people in an open roofed steamcar, going down Main Street. It should be easy to spot. Any more orders?" He listened for a moment then signed off with a relieved sigh. His part was done. He did not know who the Redman Captain and his crew were, nor did he care to. As enemies of the White Lady, they were all soon dead anyway.

# AUTHOR'S NOTE

Thank you for reading *Wind Dancer*. I hope you enjoyed the crew, the ship and their story. I'd really appreciate it if you could take a moment to review the book at your place of purchase. Your comments mean the world to me.

For more information about my writing projects join my mailing list at impishpress.com or visit my writing blog http://ravenbond.com. In thanks, I will send you a free story or the excerpt of the next project.

I am working on the final stage of the next book in the series. It will come out in the spring of 2015.

Raven Bond, Yule 2014

Author blog – http://ravenbond.com

# RAVEN BOND REVIEWS

## STRONG MAGIC REVIEWS

Mystery wrapped in enigma—This is one of my favorite styles of writing - there's enough detail to make it interesting and enough left to your imagination to make it personal. The characters are enigmatic, even to each other and the small reveals along the way give the story an intimate feeling. The Steam aspect is subtle and the magic is unique. The pacing and careful use of language are reminiscent of R.A MacAvoy. I look forward to the next installment! Bring it on, Raven Bond!

Wonderfully rollicking good fun! —I give this book 5 Stars! Lots of fun! A wonderful mix of Steampunk and magic and general Victorian landscape. Set in Victorian Age Hong Kong, surrounded by the works of Steampunk as well as a very strong magical presence. Raven has incorporated some really fun elements as well as some really fun witty banter. I recommend this to anyone who is into Steampunk, Magic and/or the Victorian era!

Too good to put down—charge your device! This is a page turner. I'm writing this review whilst waiting for my device to charge so that I can get back to the action, I'm sure it is going ahead without me. The pace is breathtaking from the very first scene. The writing is tight and very well crafted. I am right in the scene with the characters. Murder and Mystery in a Steampunk setting what more can you ask for?

Fresh take on the steampunk mystery—This is the first work I have read by Mr. Bond and I loved it! I enjoy all things mystery and steam punk and had felt like I'd read everything. Hong Kong is a fresh new location in the Steampunk genre and adds an exotic flavor to the mystery. The characters are strong- each has a full personality and the feeling of a life beyond the current book and stories all their own; the mystery aspect was solid and interesting. Mr. Bond has a knack for just the right amount of detail in a scene- enough to set the stage and let your mind fill it out- and for creating characters that I can't wait to meet again.

Strong Alchemy—Many of the characters in Strong Magic know a great deal about alchemy, the mystical art of combining disparate elements in order the produce a substance with rare and wondrous qualities. They are not alone in their expertise.

In this new work, Raven Bond blends ingredients of espionage adventures, murder mysteries, historical thrillers, science fiction, occultism and fantasy into a singular new substance with a gleaming, brassy, steampunkish glow

# STRONG ADEPT REVIEWS

Ill met in scarlet—Durable fictional pairings need an attention-grabbing starting point, a sharp, addictive exploration of the convergence of their paths. And that, ladies and gentlemen, is precisely what Raven Bond delivers here. As an introduction to the Magica sequence, Strong Adept briskly draws us into an enigmatic variation of our universe, into its exotic, curiously familiar cultures, and, most importantly, into the intriguing dynamic between his two charismatic protagonists.

Perfectly paced backstory and introduction—A fast paced stand alone short story that teases you sufficiently to want the next book(and then the next). This is the perfect introduction to Owen Strong's world. It enhances the storyline of Strong Magic in subtle ways.

Excellent book— I was unable to put this down. I recommend this to everyone. Mr. Bond is an excellent wordsmith. I can't wait for the next chapter.

Steampunk + magic = nonstop read—Fun prequel to Strong Magic, can be read before or after the first novel with equal enjoyment!

# BOOKS BY RAVEN BOND

## STEAMPUNK MAGICA SERIES

Strong Adept

Strong Magic

Strong Justice*

## THE SECRET WAR STEAMPUNK SERIES

Wind Dancer

Alien Devices*

*2015 releases